Confessions of a Nerdy Girl

Diary #2

UNLUCKY THIRTEEN

by Linda Rey

www.NerdyGirlBooks.com

Confessions of a Nerdy Girl: Top Secret is a work of fiction. Names, characters, places, and incidents either are the product of the author's imagination or are used fictitiously. Any resemblance to actual persons, living or dead, events, or locales is entirely coincidental.

Copyright © 2019 Pretty Bird Literary

ISBN 978-1-949557-04-6

Cover art by www.fiverr.com/Nizar86

Summary: From her constant humiliations at middle school, to the challenges of puberty, a self-professed nerdy girl shares her secrets in a diary dedicated to the mother who gave her up for adoption.

For Vita and Gracie

CONTENTS

JUNE 15, 7:15 P.M.

Dear M,

Have you ever had a question or a thought get stuck in your brain?

I mean seriously stuck, like, peanut butter on the roof of your mouth — stuck. Or gum on the bottom of your shoe — stuck. Or that gosh-awful, please-make-it-stop, 'Baby Shark' song that infiltrates every one of the 86 billion nerve cells in your brain until you want to tear the ears off your head to make it stop — stuck.

Well, I've had a question that's decided to camp out in my brain for a while now, so I'm just going to "bite the bullet," as my dad says, and ask—

Did you give me away when I was a baby because I was ugly, or was it because having a kid wasn't as fun as you thought it would be? Olivia, my adoptive sister, thinks you gave me away because of how hideous I was, but I don't know if I believe that. I've seen plenty of ugly babies out in public with their moms, and the moms seem to go all gaga crazy over them as if they were the cutest kids on the entire planet.

I think whoever said, "love is blind," was on to something. I have a feeling that if you love someone, or some THING, like your dog or cat or pet tarantula or whatever your deal is, that even if they aren't cute by "today's standards," it's more about the FEELINGS you have for them than what they look like. (Because, let's get real, if you're going on looks alone, how can ANYONE love snakes and spiders??)

If you gave me away because of how I looked, was it because you couldn't afford to fix my cleft lip? (I apologize if talking about money crosses a "boundary." My dad — yes, I know, TECHNICALLY, he's my "adoptive dad," but he sure feels REAL to me — says that it's rude to discuss money, religion, or politics with someone unless you know them really well, and even then, it's dicey.) I don't know how much the operation costs to correct a cleft lip or palate, but I bet it costs a lot!

The surgery is called a CHEILOPLASTY, and, according to my dad, it's pretty common. (My dad assisted with my surgery, before he was my dad, back when he was just "Dr. Ted," the dentist who came to our orphanage every few months to check our teeth.)

Not to gross you out or anything, but here's how

they do the surgery: First, the surgical team makes an incision on each side of the "split" on the lips or the cleft, as it's called, to create two flaps. Next, they pull the sides together, sew the cleft shut, and voilà—no more cleft! It leaves a scar, but mine isn't as bad now as it was a few years ago, and my dad says it will continue to fade as I get older.

My dad also says I can thank the state of Illinois for my surgery because it was done while I still lived at the orphanage, so I didn't get a bill or anything, in case you were wondering. And I gotta say, now that I'm older, I really appreciate what a "gift" the surgery was in helping to improve my looks. Not that I'm some totally hot babe, but I look waaayyyy better. (I'm even tempted to send the governor of Illinois a long overdue thank you card! Would that be weird?)

According to Olivia, on a scale of 1 to 10, I'm like a 2.5 or 2.75, max. Personally, I think I'm at least a 3 if I factor in my quick wit and the large diameter sizes of my bubble gum bubbles. (That has to account for something, right?)

Oh! Gotta go! It's father/daughter night, and my dad is taking me out for ice cream! I love me some Rocky Road!!!!!

Until next time,

Willa

JUNE 21, 10:10 P.M.

Dear M,

I think I need to explain to you the "family dynamics" of my adoptive family, the Shisbeys. (And I promise, this is not meant to make you feel bad about ~~deserting~~ ... ~~abandoning~~ ... I mean, **leaving** me one year and one day after my birth.)

First, there's my dad, Theodore, but everyone calls him Ted. He's super easygoing, and I know he loves me a lot.

Then there's Diane, my adoptive mom, who I have to call "Mom" to her face (some unwritten adoption "rule," I think), but who will never be more to me than the woman who is married to my dad, for reasons I'll explain in a bit. Unlike my dad, who hugs me and shows affection, Diane is super ... I don't know ... distant, I guess, is how I'd describe her. (Not to everyone, though. That's just how she acts towards me. To other people she puts on her "PRECIOUS," "DEAREST," "DARLING" persona, like she's some fading movie star from the 1950s.)

Next in the lineup is Oliva—their lone, freakishly beautiful, and dumb as a box of rocks daughter. I know that last part sounds mean and super judgy, but even Oliva acknowledges her cerebral limitations. As Olivia says, if one can choose to be dumb, pretty, and blond, over smart, homely, and mousey—one should choose option A., because, according to Olivia, "it's a scientific fact that blonds have more fun." (See what I mean? The girl is clueless!)

Last in the Shisbey family lineup is me, the adopted kid diagnosed with the rare memory condition, Highly Superior Autobiographical Memory, or "H-SAM" for short, that allows me to recall with computer accuracy every day of my crummy life since the day you last saw me. According to the doctors, I'm the thirteenth documented case in the **entire** world. (Yay, me! … Not!!! That just makes me UNLUCKY THIRTEEN.)

Whatever I am, it's not enough for Diane to love me as Olivia continues to remind me on a weekly basis. And if what Olivia said is true, Diane recently called the orphanage (almost 8 years after the fact!) to ask about their "return policy."

"BUMMER," Olivia said. "All sales at that place are final."

Say what?

Sometimes I hear my dad and Diane argue about me. (Let me say for the record that my dad is "Team Willa" all the way.)

The first time I heard my dad and Diane argue about me, I had gotten up to go pee in the night, and I heard my name. So, I stood on the other side of the door to listen. It was a Wednesday night, six months after I came to live with the Shisbeys. My dad and Diane were in their bedroom, and my dad sounded mad, asking Diane why she never kisses me goodnight, like she does Olivia each night.

"I just can't seem to warm up to her, Ted," I heard Diane say. "I want to, but I can't. She's just so ..." It took a few seconds for Diane to find the right word. When she did, the word was "odd." Diane, my new mom, called me "odd." Even though I fought against them, tears filled my eyes and trickled down my cheeks. "That child is just so odd," Diane said again, just in case my dad hadn't heard her the first time.

Then I heard Diane say she never would have agreed to the adoption if my dad hadn't taken her to see the musical "Annie" for their wedding anniversary, just weeks before he asked her to agree to the adoption. Diane told my dad she got "swept up in the moment," thinking of all of those precious raggedy orphan kids washing dirty dishes while singing their little hearts out. (Her words.)

The night after I listened to them talk about me (and cried for hours after), I came up with a plan to get Diane to like me. I found a tattered flannel nightgown of Olivia's in the rag drawer in the garage, and after dinner, I shrugged it on over my clothes and came into the kitchen belting out my best rendition of "It's The Hard-Knock Life" while clearing the dirty dishes from the table.

Diane wasn't impressed. In fact, she seemed mad, and she told me to stop acting silly. I must have made an impression on my dad, though, because he started crying. Not because he was sad, but because he was laughing so hard, he just about fell off of his chair.

So even though I consider my dad my "DAD" and my "FATHER" (sorry, but I do), Diane will never be more than Olivia's mom or the woman married to my dad.

I'm gonna sign off for now. I'm feeling sad (and also a little sorry for myself), and I don't want to be a downer.

Willa

JUNE 24, 9:32 A.M.

Special
=DAY=

Dear M,

Guess what??

I have the greatest news EVER to share with you! Are you ready?

Here goes ...

For the first time in my life, I can officially report that I, Wilhelmina Eugenia Shisbey, have an HONEST TO GOODNESS BFF!

HURRAY!!

In the off chance that you don't know what BFF stands for, like, if maybe you live in some faraway country or maybe you only have adult friends who don't speak in abbreviations or acronyms, BFF stands for Best Friends Forever.

And I know I shouldn't overthink it, especially since having a BFF for the first time is pretty special, but I'm sort of questioning the commitment of that second "F," the one that stands for "FOREVER."

Seriously? **FOREVER?** Like, UNTIL THE **END** OF **ALL** ETERNITY?!

That seems an awful lot to ask of someone who's still at a point in her life that she's never even been to a PG-13 movie by herself.

My new BFF's name is Marley, and she's flesh and blood. (I have to mention that she's flesh and blood because I "made up" my first BFF. And I don't mean that I overinflated the closeness of our relationship when in reality we just attended the same school or something. I mean I pretended she was an honest-to-goodness real person, which she wasn't.)

I don't want you to get the idea that I'm a total liar, but how is it possible to go through life without a BFF? It didn't seem fair that some kids get a bunch of them, and I couldn't scrounge up a single one.

I told the kids at my old school in Chicago that I'd met Tatiana, or "Tati" as I liked to call her, at summer camp in the Poconos the summer of 6th grade. I told them Tati and I were still super close and we wrote to each other at least once a week. I explained that when you have ONE really spectacular friend, then one friend is plenty. No need to be greedy, right?

It was dicey — the lie. I see that now. Because (A) I've never been to the Poconos, a mountain region in northeast Pennsylvania encompassing 2,400 square miles and home to rolling mountain terrain, breathtakingly beautiful waterfalls, and 170 miles of winding rivers, according to the

Pennsylvania Tourist Bureau website.

(B) I've never been to summer camp. (No way! No how! You can't make me! All that dirt and those bugs, not to mention having to sleep in the same room with a bunch of random strangers.)

Ewww...

And (C) I never gave Tati a body. Like, I mean, she was more of a THOUGHT than a person, if that makes sense. She was formless, sort of like a ghost maybe, although a ghost with long flowing hair.

So here's my problem by not having a well-thought-out lie: The first time someone asked me what Tati looked like, I spaced. I even had to repeat the question. "What does Tatiana look like?" Then, to buy myself some time to come up with a description, I asked a second time. "You're asking me what Tatiana LOOKS LIKE??"

"Yeah, stupid," Allie Rice said to me. "Are you deaf or something? What does your BFF look like?"

And because I had heard "Let it Go" that morning on a TV commercial (in my opinion, another stupid brain-sucking song that lodges and refuses to "let go"), I described Tatiana as ELSA, complete with her long platinum blonde braid and her slinky and totally inappropriate for cold weather blue dress.

It's fair to say no one believed me that I had a beautiful friend named Tatiana who dresses in floor length satin and blue gauze, and I can't say that I blame them.

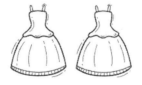

(Note to self: The next time I come up with an imaginary friend, I need to IMAGINE some proper clothes for them to wear!)

I know what you're probably thinking. You're thinking I'm a PATHETIC LOSER!!! Because, come on, who else but a total loser has had ZERO human being REAL PEOPLE BFFs by the time they're almost 13? Not many, I'd guess.

My new bestie's name is Marley May Applegate. She's not only the student body president at my new middle school but also the editor of the school paper, "The Armada," so she's well-liked by just about everybody! (Some kids may have ulterior motives because middle school kids are TOTAL media hounds. EVERYONE want to get their picture in the newspaper, so they totally suck up to her.)

I'm so happy right now that I want to pinch myself and make sure I'm not dreaming! I can't believe such a great person would want to besties with ME, but I'm not going to "look a gift horse in the mouth," as my dad says, which in some confounded way means that you're not supposed to be ungrateful when you receive a gift.

I even love Marley's name. Marley May Applegate. It has a sing-songish quality about it, sort of like the beginning of a double Dutch jump rope song, don't you agree?

Marley May Applegate

Standing by her house front gate

She's so smart

She's so cool

She does really well in school

It needs some work because I've used "gate" in two consecutive stanzas, but you get the idea.

Marley told me she hates her name. She says she'd trade me names in a heartbeat. I told her she's crazy. Marley May versus WILHELMINA EUGENIA?

SERIOUSLY? Not even close!!

Sorry to say this, M, but I just have to ask — WHAT ON EARTH were you THINKING when you named me that?!! You named me, right? That's what I've been told. Although that's about ALL.

Not how old you were or what nationality or what you looked like. All I know is my birth mother named me Wilhelmina Eugenia, and

SUPPOSEDLY the Wilhelmina part was after some famous model in the 1960s, which is hard to believe, considering I was born partially deformed. Or maybe the correct words are partially "unformed," since a cleft lip happens when the two separate areas of the face don't join and fuse correctly when the baby is still inside the mom.

I really doubt that when they handed you a baby with a messed-up face from a birth defect that you immediately thought, "Hey, I think I'll name my disfigured kid after a supermodel."

Not to keep harping on it, but did you come up with the name last minute, or was it something you already had picked out? Like, is there a Grandma Wilhelmina (or maybe you call her Grandma Mina?) on yours or my birth father's side?

I guess it could have been worse because I also found the names Wateen and Wafaa listed on the W page of the 1001 BABY NAMES book in a box in the garage filled with Olivia's baby stuff, so I guess I shouldn't complain too much.

Oh! That's it for now! My dad just told me that Marley is at the front door. Yay!!!

Willa

JULY 1, 10:05 P.M.

Dear M,

I want to tell you a little more about Marley. First off, Marley is super small. Petite, I guess, is a better way to describe her because she's small all over, not just short for her age. Marley is almost a year younger than I am. She just turned twelve even though we'll both be starting 8th grade soon. That's because Marley's so smart she skipped a grade. And I mean SUPER smart!!

Marley is a member of Mensa. In case you're not familiar, Mensa is the largest and oldest high IQ society in the world. It's an organization open to people who score at the 98th percentile or higher on a standardized, supervised IQ intelligence

test. The important word there is "supervised."
It's to make sure the applicants don't cheat by
Googling for the answers on their phones or
reading the answers off of the insides of their
forearms, the words hidden underneath their
long-sleeved shirts, like Olivia does on the days
she's tested on questions more challenging than
her name and eye color.

Marley's mom, Doctor Applegate, said that
Marley could "test out" and be in high school if
she wanted, but that the family feels it's
important for Marley to have a "regular
childhood." Which is a good thing because
Marley looks like a child with her dreadlock
pigtails and her rainbow-colored wardrobe.
Truth be known, and don't tell Marley I said this
cuz she gets this a lot and she totally hates it,
but Marley is a dead ringer for Doc McStuffins.
Do you know who that is? Doc McStuffins is an
animated character on TV who fixes toys with
the help of her toy friends.

Marley is half-black. Her mom is Jamaican, and her dad is "Floridian," which is just a fancy way of saying that he was born in Florida. Mr. Applegate says he's a "mutt" and a mixture of "ish" nationalities: British, Scottish, Irish, and maybe some Spanish. But I don't see that part because he had blond hair and blue eyes.

Marley has this brown beautiful skin that looks just like velvet. I'm not kidding. It totally does. I even asked Marley if I could touch her skin when I met her. And not in some freaky racist way (I've seen brown skin before.), but to see if Marley's skin felt as soft as it appeared.

The fact Marley said yes and didn't think I was a total nutcase for asking, well, let's just say ... I knew it was the beginning of a beautiful friendship...

Until next time,

Willa

JULY 2, 9:45 P.M.

Dear M,

Sorry about ending so abruptly last time. "Nature called," as they say.

I wanted to give you some backstory on how I met Marley, in case you were wondering. I mean, it could have been so many places, right? The mall, the soda shop, the cinema ...

Ha! Just kidding. That was my attempt at humor. I'm pretty much a lonely hermit without a life outside of the four walls of my bedroom. Besides, our local mall has recently closed, and soda shops have been extinct for decades. Do people even go OUT to the movies anymore? It seems to me, if you wait long enough, you can eventually watch all the movies on Netflix for free. (And while wearing your pajamas, I might add.)

I met Marley when she came up to me at the Friendship Bench on my first day at Triton Middle School. The Friendship Bench is sort of a hook-up point for those of us on the OUTSIDE of the cool kid circle. Basically, you just sit on a wooden bench, colorfully painted, and wait for someone to come and say hello to you. It feels a bit like being the new dog at an animal shelter, where you put on your sad puppy face and whimper a bit, hoping that someone feels sorry enough to take you home.

It can be demoralizing at first, but they promote the heck out of it in the "New Kid on Campus Handbook," the booklet you get when you enroll at Triton. There's even an entire section dedicated to it: how it was started by a fifth grader named Acacia (pronounced Ah-Kay-Sha) Woodley because of her personal struggles with bullies on account of being born without complete arms and how now it's become a national MOVEMENT.

The handbook calls The Friendship Bench "a place for HELP, SUPPORT and COMFORT." I gotta say it takes some courage, and when I sat there for the first time (FYI, sometimes it takes a few tries to get noticed), I tried NOT to look like a TOTAL DORKY LAME-O as I ate my lunch ALL ALONE and waited for SOMEONE … ANYONE? … ANYONE? … HeLLOOooo! … to come and acknowledge my pitiful and solitary existence before the end of this century or before the next bell rang, whichever came first.

Tick Tock, Tick Tock

After Marley introduced herself to me with a handshake, surprisingly firm for someone so small, she gave me a quick tour of the campus, pointing out where all the girls' bathrooms are, telling me to avoid the one on the first floor of the science building because of an unfortunate sulfuric acid prank involving stall #4, and explaining how the plumbing is now all jacked up and the entire bathroom smells of rotten eggs.

Marley was nice enough to give me the 411 on all the "IT" kids at Triton, which kids are nice and which kids to look out for. And then, because Marley is almost as OCD as I am, she wrote a Who's Who list to get me up to speed, taping it to the inside of my binder so I didn't accidentally try to have a conversation with a popular cool kid and endanger LIFE and LIMB! (Those are my words. What Marley said was, "So you don't get your feelings hurt when you try to talk to them and they pretend you don't exist.")

Marley also said I was at "a terrible disadvantage" because most of the kids at Triton had all grown up together, so the cliques were super cemented from way back in elementary school. Then she smiled her dazzling smile and added, "Not that an independent thinker like yourself would ever want to be one of THEM." (Which I think was Marley's nice way of saying she'd be disappointed in me if I even tried.)

So here's Marley's list and the rules regarding "The Major Players" at my middle school.

WARNING! DO NOT ATTEMPT TO ENGAGE THE FOLLOWING:

Dakota Duncan: #1 Triton "Mean Girl" (Blonde-haired, blue-eyed bimbette with lower-than-average IQ. Girlfriend of Cody Cassidy.)

*Methods of Torture include: General Snark, Backstabbing, Ridicule, and Baseless Rumor-Mongering. Subject has perfected the "Duncan Eye Narrow," usually presented with a sneer and rude remarks.

Dallas Duncan: Dakota's identical twin sister

(But with a slightly higher IQ, hinting at the possibility that they are really just fraternal twins who are freakishly alike.) Dallas is the unofficial president of the unofficial fan club, "Dakota's Darlings." You can find them holding their daily meetings at the COOL KIDS TABLE at lunch while plotting their next coup.

Hallie Rice: Vice President of Dakota's Darlings

Keiran Jacobs: Secretary of Dakota's Darlings

Brylee Harris: Treasurer of Dakota's Darlings

Kirby McIntyre: Media Manager of Dakota's Darlings. (Snap Chat and Instagram mostly.)

NOTE: All club positions are subject to change depending on … well, anything and nothing — as far as I can tell.

MAY ENGAGE:

Cody Cassidy: Most popular student at Triton. (He's really nice, and he's super cute. Frankly, I don't know what he sees in Dakota.)

Armada Staff: Omar, Amir, Rebekka, and Audrey. Easily identifiable by the "Armada Staff" lanyards and badges worn around their necks during regular school hours.

All teaching staff and faculty: (But steer clear of Mrs. Maroney in the front office around the 5th of every month, and for a few days after that, if you know what I mean.)

All 6th graders: (They're too young to be under Dakota's spell.)

7th grade boys: (Probably under Dakota's spell, but refreshingly naïve about social pecking order.)

7th grade girls: Use caution when trying to engage. May proceed if they are still using regular backpacks and not designer "book bags" like the members of Dakota's Darlings. The book bags are a dead giveaway that they are now M.I.T. — Members-in-Training.)

IT'S ANYONE'S GUESS:

1. Dylan Russell

2. Jax Johnson

3. Braden Becker

(Note: It depends on if they are: (A) With Cody — in which case you may engage. (B) Alone — which is usually also OK. Or (C) Somewhere within hearing distance of Dakota, in which case I wouldn't chance it because they pretty much hang on Dakota's every word and secretly pray for Cody to come down with a bad case of acne or halitosis—giving them a chance with her.)

Then Marley told me that her list was only a GUIDE and that I should just "go for it" and say Hi to everyone, telling me that "fear has no place at Triton Middle School." (Before adding, "Neither does bullying, but unfortunately that's been an uphill battle.")

Yikes!! Would you look at the time?? (That's a saying people use when they're late for something. I don't mean you need to look at it. Plus, when you think about it, no one can LOOK at time. They can look at a clock or their watch or their phone or something, showing a number REPRESENTING our INTERPRETATION of measurements defined by the movements of astronomical objects — but it is IMPOSSIBLE to "LOOK at time!") Just sayin'.

Anyhow, I need to stop for now and get some shut-eye. I have a big day tomorrow doing nothing.

Until next time,

Willa

SEPTEMBER 3, 9:29 P.M.

Dear M,

Sorry about the long lapse in writing, but honestly, my life is sooooo boorrriiiinnnggg, that there wasn't much to say. UNTIL TODAY!

You WILL NOT believe what happened today! Honestly, it was funny, GROSS, and mortifying all at the same time.

To sum it up in three words, your daughter is "OFFICIALLY A WOMAN," which I'm sure you know is a super corny way of saying that I got my period for the very first time.

I have to say, M, I don't know that I've ever missed you more than I did today. My dad did his best to help, he really did, but sometimes a girl just needs her mother.

I thought "IT" might happen soon (getting my period) since I'll be 13 on my next birthday. When I asked Olivia what to expect, she just blew me off and said it was gross and I'd hate it and ask her mom to explain it. And there was NO WAY I'd do that because Diane was no help WHATSOEVER when I needed my first (and potentially — LAST) bra, passing the baton to my dad and making him take me, which was even WORSE than it sounds!

Sooo embarrassing!

SO, instead, I did what every girl in my situation does, and I went to my trusted school nurse for advice.

JUST KIDDING! HA!

Do schools even have nurses anymore? With all the budget cuts, we might get an LVN to stop by once a month to log some necessary clinical hours and to bandage a scraped knee or something while she's there, but nurses in middle schools are as rare as gym towels these days from what I see.

What I really did was Google the words "WHAT TO EXPECT FOR YOUR FIRST PERIOD," and it gave me 7,350,000 results, starting with the info (below) highlighted inside one of those boxes at the top of the page and obviously just meant for British girls because it said this:

"Usually you will notice the arrival signs of **your first period** when you go to the **LOO**. There may be some dark **COLOURING** in **your undies**. This is the menstrual blood of **your first period** – so congrats! Menstrual blood is the lining of the womb that has done its job and is now clearing out of the body."

The "congrats" was a bit over the top, if you ask me. It's not as if a girl has much of a say in the matter. I don't think a period is something you accomplish by will or effort.

Another website gave me a checklist of things that have to happen BEFORE you even get your period. They're, like, prerequisites or something.

Here's the list:

1. Breast "buds" develop for 3-4 years prior. (They are not to be confused with the actual breasts themselves, which continue to form.)

I showed Olivia the article to see if what they were saying was true, and she said, "How would I know? I've had nice breasts as long as I can remember." Which is a total lie! I've known Olivia since the Shisbeys adopted me when I was five and Olivia was eight, and she definitely DID NOT have breasts visible to the "naked" eye back then or for years after that.

After reading the article, Olivia agreed that I'm definitely still in the BUD stage. She even said that because I'm such a loser, there's a good chance I'll stay in the bud stage and never get to the BLOOM part. And then because she's Olivia, and Olivia's a cretin, she now insists that the entire family must call me "Buddy." (Get it? "Bud"—Buddy.)

2. Pubic hair will appear. First, it will be soft and thin, gradually becoming coarser. FYI: Yes, I have some, but I won't bore you with the scraggly sparse details.

(Forewarning: This next part is sort of disgusting...)

3. Girls will experience "vaginal discharge." It can be white or yellowish. (They suggest a thin pad or panty liner for "comfort." FYI: They neglected to say that sometimes it feels as if you've wet your pants.)

Then the site explained about PMS: the headaches, the zits, the depression, and the anger. And that's why I thought MAYBE "the curse" was coming soon because I've had a pizza face full of zits and I've been super depressed. (But Olivia says I have pizza face because I have pizza STOMACH — as in, I ate almost an entire pepperoni by myself last week — and I'm depressed because my dad moved me to California and away from Chicago and all of my friends. Then she corrected herself, and she said, "Oh, that's right. I forgot. You didn't HAVE any friends to move away FROM," before laughing her fool head off.)

OK, so now you're up to speed on the backstory, and I can tell you the humiliating part.

Diane and Olivia had gone to get their nails done, and I was at home with my dad watching cartoons. For clarification, I mean that I was the one watching cartoons. My dad was mulching in the garden or doing something DAD-ish outside in the yard. I had plans to go to swim at Marley's pool, but that wasn't for another hour.

I was (NERD ALERT!) watching a rerun of "The Big Bang Theory" when I felt this crampy sensation and then a rush of warmth inside my underwear. Immediately I ran to the bathroom, thinking it was maybe just more of #3 on "The What to Expect List," when to my horror, I discovered it was RED! And, so, OK, looking at it now, it wasn't GALLONS, like the amounts of blood in a slasher movie or anything, but because it was coming out of my body and I've been known to pass out from little more than a skinned knee, I totally FREAKED!! I'm not kidding. I started SCREAMING for my dad from my seated position on the toilet. (Or the LOO, according to Brits.)

I could hear my dad's garden clogs running on the tile and him yelling, "I'M COMING,

WILLA!" And then he tried to open the bathroom door in order to get to me, which I'd locked.

And I know you'll think I'm a total wuss, but I started crying when I saw the blood. Blubbering like nobody's business while my dad pounded on the door and wanted to know what was wrong.

"I … I … star … star …ted … my … my … per … i … od," I sort of hiccupped because I was crying so hard.

And you want to know what my dad's response was?

SILENCE!! As in ZIP-A-DEE-DOO-DAH.

NADA!

ZILCH!

My words were met by TOTAL SILENCE. I couldn't even hear my dad BREATHING!! It was like he had died or something.

"Dad?" I said. "Dad, are you there?"

"I'm here, Willa," he said. And his voice sounded weird. Almost like he was choked up or was maybe even CRYING, too, if you can believe that!

"What do I DO?" I asked him, and even through the door, I heard his heavy sigh.

"Do you want me to come in?" he asked, his voice soft, but now that I think about it was probably more the sound of "dread" than anything else.

"NO WAY!" I yelled at him, mortified, and then in a nicer tone I said, "Just tell me what to do."

The doctor part of him seemed to kick in (He's a dentist but still.), and he started barking out orders. "First, check under the sink and see if there are any feminine pads while I'll go check our bathroom," he said, meaning the bathroom he and Diane share next to their bedroom down the hall.

I wadded some toilet tissue and jammed it in my underwear before pulling up my pants and hunting in the cupboards.

No luck. The only feminine product was a "Feminine SPRAY," whatever the heck that is.

"Any luck?" My dad called through the door after a minute or two.

"No. What about you?" I called back.

"Uhhh... I think so," he said. And by this time I was PRAYING for Olivia and Diane to come home. At least they were GIRLS even if they weren't the most helpful.

"Whaddaya mean?" I said. (Seriously, it wasn't a

hard question. It had to be either YES or NO.)

"Well, sweetie, I found a few that might work. But... uhh... do you need a 'Liner,' this one says, or something called an 'Ultra-thin'?" I heard the muted sound of tearing cardboard and then what sounded like my dad shuffling a deck of cards. "Wait, wait! Here's one that says 'Flexi-wing.'" And then more to himself than to me, "Hmmm...?" Before saying, "Ohhh! I get it now. It has wings. Do you want the one with wings? ... Nope, wait! Here's another one. This one says it's for overnight. Do you need that one?"

Liner? ... Ultra-thin? ... Flexi-wing? ... Overnight????? Ahhhh!!

The choices overwhelmed me.

"How would I know?" I said, and my voice cracked as the tears dripped off my nose. I used my sleeve to wipe the tears and the snot from my face.

I think my dad could tell I was crying because his voice got super soft, and he said, "If you open the door, sweetie, I'll just hand you the bunch of them, and you can choose."

"No way! I'm not opening the door!" I told him, and I slid to the ground with my back to the door and basically had a total meltdown. "WHY IS THIS HAPPENING TO ME NOW?" I yelled out.

Why? Why?? Why???

I heard my dad clear his throat. In fact, he cleared it twice before saying, "Well, it's like this, Willa. When a girl reaches puberty, hormones cause the lining of the uterus to build... and.. if... uh... the ... uh, egg..."

Ewww! No! I did NOT need my dad going all

birds and bees on me. I just meant I wanted to know why it was happening in THAT moment when there was no one else home except for my DAD. All that other stuff I learned, like, back in the 5th grade when we had to watch those dumb animated videos in health class.

I slid my hand through the opening at the bottom of the door and wiggled my fingers. "Just push them through," I said, sighing.

And one by one, my dad pushed them underneath the door, little folded packages, slithering along the tile in succession, like cars on a train. Except for the last one. The HUMONGOUS one the size of a folded Sunday newspaper. That one got stuck underneath the door, and I had to unwedge it with the stick end of the toilet plunger.

The story ends there because Diane and Olivia came home and my dad skedaddled faster than you can say PUBERTY. It was Olivia (if you can believe it) who came to my rescue by using a hairpin to unlock the door to the bathroom and invade my privacy, where she proceeded to tell me to quit being such a baby and that the Ultra-thin was more than adequate for a noobie.

Anyway, that's all for now. I gotta go. My dad's taking me out to dinner to celebrate the BIG DEAL.

Yours in womanhood,

Willa

SEPTEMBER 21, 6:17 P.M.

Dear M,

It's back to school for Willa Gene (That's what Olivia calls me when she is mad at me, and basically, she's mad at me 24/7.).

I was hoping I'd become an A-LISTER since becoming friends with Marley, but sadly that's not the case. So far, I've been hit in the back of the head by half an egg salad sandwich (extra mayo) and intentionally tripped TWICE when I walked back to my seat in second period (Suspect is male, torn jeans, size 7 shoe.), and it's been less than two weeks since the start of school. Grrr!!

Today I took part in something called "beach cleanup day." Beach cleanup is pretty much just what you'd expect. You walk around the beach picking up trash that slobs have left behind. I'd like to report that it was a huge success, but I'd be lying. Not only was the beach NOT cleaned to my high standards, (HA!) but I made a total idiot of myself in front of most of the kids in my 8th grade class when I fainted after getting stung by a jellyfish.

Turns out, California does NOT have poisonous HUMAN-KILLING jelly fish, but I didn't know it at the time, and I thought it was a BOX JELLYFISH, one of the deadliest jellyfish on the planet. (FYI: Did you know that a jellyfish is 95% water and has no brain? Or that it eats and poops out of the same opening?? Well, now you know!)

Anyhoo... This is what happened...

I was walking along the edge of the water, hot as heck in my long pants and long-sleeved shirt, because I DID NOT KNOW it can be a MILLION degrees at the beach in California in September! (I must have missed the school memo suggesting shorts or a sundress, which there is NO WAY I would have done anyway with my gross hairy and white legs!!)

As I was saying ... I was walking along the water's edge, carrying my trash bag while dressed for the SNOW and sweating like a banshee, so much that my glasses were all fogged and I could hardly see, when I spotted a plastic baggie at the water's edge. Cody, the cute surfer boy from Marley's list and a member of the environmental group that sponsored the event, told us to be on the lookout for plastic as our #1 priority. So as you can imagine, I was on a mission to find every piece of plastic around so that Cody would be proud of me or maybe so I'd win a prize or something.

I reached down to grab the baggie to put inside my trash bag, and as I did, I felt a horrible shooting pain in my hand! After defogging my glasses, I saw what had happened. I'd been STUNG BY A JELLYFISH masquerading as a plastic bag!! Knowing I only had a short time left to live, according to that article I read on Our Deadly Planet three years, two months, and six days ago (thanks H-SAM), I collapsed to the ground and began to crawl UP the sand and

AWAY from shore because I did NOT want to die IN the water and become a DECAYING LOG of fish food!

I guess I fainted, face up, a little up shore. Apparently, I'd hyperventilated from fear. It was Cody who found me, and he alerted the lifeguard. I don't remember it, but Marley said the lifeguard had to carry me all the way to the medical tent set up for the event, which was quite some distance.

When I regained consciousness, I was lying on a smelly cot, and Marley was looking down on me with concern.

As if it wasn't bad enough to be lying there with my ratty bra showing (because my buttons had popped off somehow during my brush with what-could-have-possibly-been death), all the kids from my class were inside the tent, too, and except for Marley and Cody, they all started making fun of me, grabbing their necks with their hands and yelling "It bit me!! It bit me!! I'M DYING! HELP! HELP!"

Then Dakota, the evilest of evil 8th graders on the face of the PLANET, fell to the sand and started to shake and twist in what I assumed was a reenactment of me fainting, but instead, looked like she was trying to sizzle like bacon. And since all those kids want to follow "Queen D.," they started to sizzle, too, until it was one big SIZZLE FEST with half-a-dozen 8th graders shaking and sizzling in the sand, their legs and arms coated with so much sand that they looked like breaded chicken tenders pieces.

Cody and Marley were nice enough to stick up for me, telling the kids to stop (not that it helped), and then the lifeguard came over and kicked them out of the tent. (Not LITERALLY, obviously, but telling them to "hit the road.") By then, my eyes were already tearing from embarrassment, and it was all I could do to blink away the tears.

I would have totally cried, too, because I was feeling majorly sorry for myself ... that I'm such a nerd, and how I've had this sucky life with my H-SAM, and how it won't let me forget the bad moments of my life, and being adopted, and my dad moving us away, but then Marley gave me this great super hero pep talk.

Did you know, M, that most of the MAJOR super heroes were ORPHANS like me? Or that they ALL were "born of tragedy," according to Marley?

This is what Marley told me:

All the X-Men—the first major ones, anyway— were mutants born with genetic anomalies that gave them great abilities. They were the first superheroes to set the stage to right human indignities.

CAPTAIN AMERICA began life as Steve Rogers, a kid who survived polio, losing his father when he was a child and his mother after he graduated high school. Steve later became known as Captain America, SUPER-SOLDIER, modeling courage and hope in the face of insurmountable foes.

CAPTAIN MARVEL was little Billy Batson, an orphan who fought against prejudice and discrimination, later becoming Captain Marvel, PROTECTOR OF THE UNIVERSE.

SUPERMAN, as we all know, and arguably the BIGGEST SUPERHERO of all time was Clark

Kent, another orphan. He used the earth's environment to activate his incredible powers to save the world. *** (On a personal note, Clark and I have matching glasses.)

BATMAN? Orphan. Bruce Wayne was just your "average Joe" (Marley's words) without any special powers but with more money than "Jehovah," (Marley's words) who dedicated his life to prevent and avenge crimes.

SPIDERMAN? Total orphan. (Although he had that really great aunt and uncle who raised him.) Peter Parker was a kid who struggled with social interaction and suffered from bullying. After Peter got bitten by the spider, he changed, and he began to use his power to protect those who couldn't protect themselves.

After Marley finished giving me the histories, I asked her if I — like Peter Parker — could eventually become stronger because of Dakota's venom. Maybe her poison would trigger some terrific strength in me I didn't know I had.

Marley said this, "The spider is the AMALGAMATION." Then she saw my look of confusion, and she dumbed it down for me. "... a REPRESENTATION of the COMBINED QUALITIES, negative ones in this case, of people like Dakota and Dallas — and your sister, too, from what you tell me. I haven't known you for long, Willa, but I believe you could possibly become the Peter Parker of our school. Wilhelmina Shisbey — SPIDER-GIRL."

"Spider-Girl," I repeated to Marley, and even

though I'm A TOTAL arachnophobe, I liked the sound of it.

Whoops!! I forgot to empty the dishwasher, and now Diane is hollering through my bedroom door that she's deducting money from my allowance. (Although how you can DEDUCT when the starting point is ALMOST ZERO is beyond me.)

Yours in arachnophobia,

Spider-Girl

OCTOBER 15, 8:08 P.M.

Dear M,

Last night, my dad told Olivia that "it's our choices in life that define us." He said it as a part of his lecture after he grounded Olivia for stealing 20 bucks from his wallet and then lying about it. Olivia's excuse on why she stole the money was, "Would you really have given me 20 bucks for a new Sephora lipstick?" Which my dad answered, "HECK, NO!" (Only he didn't say "heck.") And then Olivia's excuse on why she lied was, "I thought at YOUR AGE you'd be too old to remember how much money you had in your wallet."

That just shows you what a nitwit Olivia is because my dad only had a single $20 bill in his wallet! She may have gotten away with it if my dad had a couple hundred bucks all in twenties stuffed inside, but when you have ONE

SOLITARY $20 bill in your wallet and then suddenly have ZERO, as in, you have a TOTALLY EMPTY WALLET (with maybe the exception of a few pieces of lint stuck inside the fold), well, it's pretty clear YOU'VE BEEN ROBBED!

After the drama was over, and Olivia got sent to her room "to think about her actions," it made me think about our CHOICES, like my dad said, and what they say about us.

So, in the spirit of choices, I came up with some "Would You Rather" questions that I'll answer so you'll know how I tick, and maybe you can answer them, too (by writing them down), and we can compare someday.

1. Would you rather eat a small can of cat food or a can of dog food?

<u>My answer:</u> A can of dog food. (I don't like fish.)

2. Would you rather be completely bald or covered from head to toe with hair?

My answer: Completely bald. (You can find some cool wigs online. I especially like the pink and purple ones. And we can pencil in our eyebrows as Diane proves every morning.)

3. Would you rather always have to skip everywhere or run everywhere?

My answer: Run. (Marley is the only person I know who looks good skipping. Although to be honest, my "run" is more of a lope.)

4. Would you rather have a horse's tail or a unicorn horn?

My answer: A horse's tail. At least you can hide it in some loose-fitting pants. (FYI: I had a zit once in the middle of my forehead that could have passed for a unicorn horn.)

5. Would you rather have a pig nose or a monkey face?

<u>My answer:</u> A pig nose. (That's only ONE plastic surgery operation. Fixing an entire face would take many surgeries.)

6. Would you rather surf in shark-infested waters or jump free fall with a parachute into the Grand Canyon?

<u>My answer:</u> Jump free fall with a parachute. (I'd rather die in one flat-as-a-pancake moment than be torn to bits and eaten by JAWS.)

7. Would you rather drink all your food from a baby bottle or wear visible diapers for the rest of your life?

My answer: Baby bottle. DEFINITELY! (Two years ago, just for fun, Olivia and I spent a day drinking from baby bottles. I can't imagine it would have been nearly as fun spending the day in a diaper.)

8. Would you rather always talk in rhymes or sing instead of speak?

My answer: Talk in rhymes. (Rappers get paid big bucks for doing just that.)

9. Would you rather suffer from spontaneous shouting or unpredictable fainting spells?

My answer: Unpredictable failing spells. (People are really nice when you faint. Plus, we once had a kid in my class with Tourette's, and he'd shout

out at random moments. I know he couldn't help it, but it was pretty annoying during test time.)

10. Would you rather wear clown makeup every day for a year or wear a tutu every day for a year?

<u>My answer:</u> A tutu. (Have you NOT seen the new movie version of "IT"??! Besides, a tutu is much more versatile than you think. Not that I've ever worn a tutu, but I've SEEN people wear them. i.e. Marley Applegate.)

11. Would you rather not be allowed to wash your hands for a month or your hair for a month?

<u>My answer:</u> Hair. Because I'm a total germaphobe. (I don't think germs stick to your head, plus, hats would both hide the grease and maybe absorb some of it, too.)

12. Would you rather always have a booger in your nose that moves when you breathe in and out or a piece of food stuck between your two front teeth?

My answer: Food stuck in my teeth. (In fact, I'd rather have an ENTIRE POT ROAST stuck in my front teeth than "A BREATHER," as the kids at school call them.)

13. Would you rather live in Narnia or go to school at Hogwarts?

My answer: Live in Narnia. Honestly, it's a miracle Harry and the gang didn't wind up catatonic by graduation, what with running from constant horror for books 1 to 7 and movies 1 to 8. (Although I have to admit, some of those feasts they got to eat at holidays looked super delish.)

14. Would you rather have bad breath and body odor the entire day or be completely naked?

My answer: DEFINITELY bad breath and body odor. (And I'd be joining 75% of my classmates. Seriously, M, some of those kids must not own a toothbrush or have access to soap and water.)

15. Would you rather be invisible or be able to fly?

My answer: Fly. (I'm already invisible.)

Until next time,

Willa

OCTOBER 19, 8:59 P.M.

Dear M,

You WILL NOT believe this!! But I promise, it's true. CODY CASSIDY, "THE" MOST POPULAR BOY AT TRITON MIDDLE SCHOOL was at my house today!! And not just with one foot inside our entryway because he was selling magazine subscriptions or newspapers or something. No, he came over to see ME!!

Cody came to tutor me in math. And I'm not using the words "tutor me in math" as a phony excuse that one gives to a parent to make it APPEAR school-related, when, in reality, we're really playing Minecraft instead.

In case you haven't heard of it, Minecraft is something people call a "sandbox game" and played on a computer or phone, where you dig ("mine") and build ("craft") different 3D blocks within a large world of varying terrains and habitats. Think **virtual** LEGO bricks, but without the toe-breaking hazards when you accidentally step on one of those suckers embedded in your rug in the middle of the night when you wake up to go pee.

As I said, Cody came over to tutor me in math. If you're anything like me, you might be thinking, "Yeah, **SURE** he came over to 'tutor' you," knowing that super cute, popular, athletic, surfer boys are not usually the brightest bulbs in the chandelier.

BUT, if that's what you thought, you'd be wrong. (As was I, which goes to show you that it's not nice to stereotype people because cute people can be smart AND cute, and people who

LOOK SMART, like me, just because they wear thick glasses, can be super dumb in math. Or if not "dumb," then "mathematically challenged," for sure.)

Cody is really good in math, but for some reason he doesn't want anyone else to know. Not even the teacher. And so he intentionally messes up on his tests or doesn't hand in the work. He hasn't told me why, though.

You'd think having H-SAM would be helpful **remembering** something as simple as numbers, but you'd be wrong.

Turns out, it's only good for remembering worthless stuff, like what I had for breakfast on the first Thursday after the full moon back in August 2012 (Fruity Pebbles) or that Sunday July 25th, just a little over a month after I'd been adopted when Diane asked my dad if the orphanage had a 90-day "exchange policy" on kids. Saying that the policy should be like the mattress store, where you get to "sleep on it" for a few months before making a FINAL decision.

I think Cody only offered to help me because he felt bad about Dakota being so mean to me the day of the beach cleanup. And also, my dad's paying him to tutor me. It's not as if he came over just to hang out. But still, it's super cool that THE CUTEST BOY in the ENTIRE SCHOOL came over to see me!

Me Me Me

I can now boast that I've had the two most popular boys in my middle schools at my house.

Although with Randall Rice at my old school, the circumstances were different. Randall came in the dead of night and brought two of his friends. They covered my front yard with a year's worth of toilet paper before scrambling two dozen eggs on all the windows. As a love letter, they wrote the word "NERD" in shaving cream on the front windshield of my dad's Prius.

I know the destruction was aimed at me, but my dad's take was that Randall had a bad dental experience the last time he came for a checkup. It was Randall's way of giving my dad a bad Yelp review.

But back to Cody.

There were a few dicey, JUST KILL ME NOW moments. The first one was when Cody managed to decode the words on my calendars. I don't need to write anything down to remember it, but it's nice to have a VISUAL reminder when something good happens in my life, proof that my life doesn't perpetually stink.

I've been collecting calendars since the first month of my adoption by the Shisbeys, and I have each month taped to my wall in orderly fashion. It looks like I have a million of them, according to Cody, but in reality I only have 148.

Some of them are super small because I cut them from pages of pocket calendars. Olivia says it's creepy, me having my walls plastered with calendars instead of teenage "heartthrob" (Is that still even a THING?) posters, and if I'm not embarrassed by it, she'll be embarrassed enough for the two of us.

My entries have the basic numeric equivalents, 1 for A, 2 for B, etc., which I know is lame, but complicated enough for someone as dumb as Olivia, the only person I know who spends 2 hours a night on YouTube entertained by videos of people using laser pointers to mess with their cats.

Cody went over to my calendars, and I knew the

jig might be up (That's an old-fashioned phrase my dad uses to mean one's been "found out".) when Cody's lips started moving as he eyed each entry, smiling or frowning as he focused on certain days. He didn't say anything, so I had my fingers crossed. After a few minutes, he came over to my desk where'd I set up our work station with an extra chair from the dining room.

I guess I could just have a second diary for that stuff, but I'm trying to be "stealth" so Olivia won't go snooping around in my room looking for a diary with my innermost secrets. Not to say that this dairy isn't important, too, but I have a feeling Olivia has already read this because she said to me the other day, "Willa, you're the only person I know whose secrets are even more boring than their everyday stuff."

 Snoozer...

I gotta go. Diane is yelling that I have to wash the windows, scrub the floors, and then clean the cinders from the fireplace while Olivia dresses for the ball at the prince's castle later tonight. (JK, Olivia won't go to the ball for another week, and it's not a "ball" as much as it is a "school dance.")

love

Willa

OCTOBER 23, 10:48 P.M.

Dear M,

Tonight I ALMOST had my very first slumber party, and it was AN ABSOLUTE AND TOTAL DISASTER!!

First of all, it wasn't my idea. It was an evil plan of Olivia's in order to get back at me for something that is so small and insignificant that you'll laugh when I tell you.

Olivia was mad at me because I dressed her in the same clothes on the same days of the week since school started. And by "dressed," I don't mean to say I'm the one pulling Olivia's sweater over her head while she holds her arms up or I button her pants or something (Gross!), but I tell her WHAT she should wear on certain days so she doesn't duplicate her outfits in the same semester.

Olivia knows that having H-SAM means I can remember stuff, so when she asks me the last time she's worn an outfit she believes what I tell her. My main goal in life is to dress Olivia in the same clothes on the same day of every month of every year.

You could call it my silent war.

Because, here's a kink to H-SAM—it's AUTOBIOGRAPHICAL. Meaning — it's all about me. Unless it's something I make a point of remembering, if it doesn't have to do with me, it's not automatically stored in my memory bank.

Now, ask me what I was wearing on any day in

any year, and I could tell you with perfect accuracy.

Let's say you picked 3 years, 2 months and 7 days ago... easy peasy. I'd tell you I wore a black graphic T-shirt that Olivia had given me (read: "thrown away" because it had a tear in the seam and armpit stains) with the words "BYE FELICIA" printed across the chest. (I'd also tell you that Diane wouldn't let me wear it out of the house because she said it was "WILDY INAPPROPRIATE" for a nine-year-old.) I also had on denim jeans that came from Target and black and white Converse sneakers, I mean "tennis shoes" in California lingo.

Later that night, I wore blue plaid flannel drawstring pajama bottoms and a blue and white T-shirt with a picture of a drowsy-looking panda across the front and the words "Bearly Awake" underneath to sleep in. (The pajamas are sort of lame — if I'm being honest — but they were a Christmas gift from my dad. I pretend they're my favorite.)

But when it comes to what Olivia wore and when, I don't care enough to remember, and so when she asks if she should wear such-and-such on a particular day, I lie.

Here's an example:

Olivia: "When did I last wear my flouncy-patterned skirt with my denim vest?"

Me—lying: "It was a Wednesday, the second week in May, and you were going shopping after school with Melody. Wear the skirt, but pair it with your slouchy pink top instead."

Olivia: "Didn't I wear this blazer with my Diesel jeans just last week?"

Me—lying: "Last week? Try last YEAR. I think you must have some memory problems."

Olivia: "Rachel says I wore this same dress now three times this month."

Me—lying: "Who you gonna believe, a girl who thinks the moon landing was nothing but a fraud or your own sister?"

How did Olivia find out that I was dressing her in the same clothes?

Well, it so happens that Olivia had some project for school (or so she SAYS ... sounds suspicious to me) where she had to take a picture of herself every day for two months.

She called her fake school project, "60 Days-60 Outfits." I don't understand what ACADEMIC VALUE 60 cheesy Instagram-ish pics would have and only proves that Olivia is a conceited, self-absorbed narcissist.

Looking at it all now, what I originally thought was a foolproof plan had one serious flaw — I totally spaced and didn't factor in that pictures stored on cell phones have the TIME AND DATE! (Duh!!)

"You just wait, Willa Gene!" Olivia threatened when she finally figured it out, pointing her phone at me, her eyes narrowed into slits. "I'll get you for this. If it's the last thing I do, I WILL GET YOU, Willa!"

Olivia was as good as her word, and that's why there were 6 girls — make that 6-6-6, DEVIL GIRLS (armed with mascara wands instead of pitch forks) at my house for a slumber party tonight, and all invited by Olivia, who had sent them some dumb Evite.

Olivia had promised that in return for suffering through a night in my presence, Olivia and Blaine, her fellow cheerleader and glamazon-in-training, would reward them with beauty makeovers and a short seminar on the latest fashion trends. **Olivia's Beauty Basics: Top 10 Must Haves**

After the attendees (Dakota's Devil Darlings) arrived, I stayed in my room. NO WAY was I going to fall for Olivia's scheme, whatever it was.

But once the pizza got delivered, it lured me out of my room with the scent of pepperoni. Besides, my dad said hiding in my room was "NOT AN OPTION," and I wasn't being a very good hostess.

I told him the word he was looking for was

"HOSTAGE," not hostess, because I DID NOT INVITE THOSE GIRLS TO MY HOUSE!! (The same girls who flailed around on the sand and made fun of me after I fainted at the beach and then stuck water-logged baggies and poorly drawn pictures all over my locker!)

My dad wouldn't let me off the hook, and he forced me to join the group. By then, Olivia's Beauty Basics seminar was over, and she and Blaine had gone into MAKEOVER MODE, tweezing and shaping the eyebrows of Dakota, Dallas, Hallie, Keiran, and Kirby. Brylee didn't get hers tweezed. She said she'd need her mom's permission first, and her mom wasn't answering her phone.

I have to say, M, everyone's eyebrows looked a lot better, not nearly so bushy.

Then they all looked at me and started chanting, "WILL-A! WILL-A! WILL-A!" Meaning that it should be my turn, except for Dakota, who instead chanted, "CAT-A-PILLAR! CAT-A-PILLAR!" as a reference for my bushy eyebrows. It didn't catch on with the rest of the girls, so she quit.

They weren't going to let me off the hook, and I finally agreed to let Blaine perform the surgery. If you didn't count the swelling and the blood that dotted in some spots where Blaine plucked skin instead of hair, I didn't look half bad. In fact, for the first time in my ENTIRE LIFE, I looked good. Who would have thought that whittling down your eyebrows so you look more like Grandma and less like Grandpa would have such dramatic results?

Kirby told me that with my eyebrows tweezed and without my glasses I was "almost kinda cute," and Blaine said I looked a little like the teen actress Bailee Madison on "Good Witch," which was a major stretch but a nice compliment. Then ruining the compliment by adding, "But the young Bailee when she still had that chubby face."

Olivia's eyes tightened, and she glared at the girls when they said those nice things about me. It was easy to see that Olivia did NOT like me getting compliments, NOT ONE BIT! The night was all about Olivia getting the glory — and me being miserable because of it.

After that, things started going downhill fast.

Olivia gave me a dirty look, and then she turned towards the girls. Her voice became unnaturally soft, so it was almost a purr, or maybe it was more of a low growl, the same sound a mountain lion makes before it pounces and rips your head off.

"If you think Willa is cute now," Olivia said, "you should see the pictures of how cute she was as a BABY."

Then she glanced over at the built-in bookcases lining the opposite wall of the room, where all the photo albums are stored inside the bottom cabinets.

"Olivia, no!" I gasped, horrified, and realized her intent. Olivia planned to show them the baby book with pictures of me BEFORE my surgery when I still had my cleft lip.

"Please, Olivia, no. I beg you! Not my baby pictures," I pleaded, my voice sounding like I was about to cry (which I totally was) while sweat beaded at the back of my neck. "No, Olivia!"

But Olivia had a plan. A mean and vicious plan. And before I could stop her, she sprinted across the room and pulled open the bottom cupboard, grabbing my baby book from the second shelf. She cracked open the pages and swiftly peeled off the pictures, passing them to the girls.

Everyone's eyes got wide, and they stared in horror at the pictures of me, a homely baby with a bald head the shape of a large spaghetti squash, skin the color of raw oysters, and that wonky crossed eye. (Mine wasn't as bad as "Mad Eye Moody" in Harry Potter, but close.)

There were gasps when the girls saw the pictures, and a few covered their mouths with their hands. (To hold back the barf, maybe?) Someone said "Eww!" and Brylee had to turn her head away and try to hide her face underneath her armpit to escape the horror.

I'm sure you remember how I looked with that cleft that ran from lip to nostril. And it's not as if I was missing the bottom half of my face, the way some kids look before their clefts or palates are repaired, but in the picture, the cleft was gaping and pink and glistened with my saliva. My lips pulled sideways in a lopsided grin, revealing those teeth I'd grown, as pointed as a poodle's.

"I hate you!" I screamed at Olivia, hot tears stinging my eyes. And I ran from the room to my father, begging him to home school me, so I wouldn't ever have to face those girls again and see their horrified expressions, knowing that whether it was two months or two years from now, the memory of how I looked when I still belonged to you would be seared on their brain.

And then, to make things even worse, if you can imagine THAT, Olivia found the hat that Cody had left behind when he came to tutor me (although how she found it buried underneath my pillow, I'll never know), and she came out and said in a phony sweet voice, "Willa, isn't this Cody's hat? He must have left it behind the other day when he was in your BEDROOM." And she said the word "bedroom" really loudly, like there was something sinister about my bedroom, when, in reality, it's the only room in our house with a desktop computer and an actual desk that a chair can slide under.

Dakota's eyes were about to pop out of her head, and her mouth dropped open when she saw that hat. I guess Cody never mentioned to her that he's tutoring me in math. After Dakota recovered from the shock, she tossed her hair (Dakota's a big hair-tosser, but I have to admit that if I had her silky long blond hair, I'd probably be a big hair tosser, too.) ...

Anyway, after Dakota tossed her hair over her shoulder, she did this cat-hunching-its-back sort of thing, and she added a "death stare." In case you're not familiar with it, a death stare is where someone squints their eyes at you and makes a mean face while loudly breathing through their noses. Then Dakota whispered some words under her breath, which I'm willing to bet was some kind of evil incantation or hex or something aimed at me, or maybe she was talking to her sister and didn't want anyone to hear, but my money is on the hex. (Which is why I currently have a rabbit's foot stuck inside my bra. Sadly, there's even room enough for a second one, with room to spare.)

The slumber-party-that-wasn't ended just after that (There was no way to recover from the drama.), and my dad drove everyone home.

On the upside, Olivia is now grounded pretty much for life.

On the downside, Olivia is grounded pretty much for life, which means she'll be home torturing me for the foreseeable future.

Yours in eminent peril,

Willa

OCTOBER 26, 7:07 P.M.

Dear M,

Today started out as one of the ALL — TIME — WORST days of my life, but if you can believe this, it ended with me getting a new friend! I guess it just goes to show you that things can change in an instant, so you need to keep "your chin up," (which means to stay brave in a difficult situation) as my dad likes to say.

It all started when I arrived at school. In hindsight, I should never have removed the rabbit's foot from my bra, but the hair was scratchy and gave me a rash, and the pointy toenails kept poking into my—

Never mind. I'm sure you get the idea.

And in case you're thinking that maybe I should have just put the rabbit's foot inside my pants pocket, well, I tried that, and with the foot in my FRONT pocket, let's just say that with that thing in the front of my pants I looked more like a "WILLIAM" Shisbey than a Wilhelmina, if you get my drift.

BACK pocket, you say? Tried that, too, until Olivia asked me if I had pooped my pants because she said it looked like I had "a load" back there, according to her.

So, anyway, like I started to say, I was walking with Marley to my locker, and I heard someone behind me say, "That's her. That's the girl in those gross pictures." It didn't take much to guess what "gross pictures" they were talking about, and as soon as I rounded the corner, I saw a group of kids clustered around my locker, laughing and making ugly faces by using their fingers to pull their lips apart to expose their gums and teeth.

When I got closer and saw the front of my locker, I wanted to faint. Or cry. Or barf. But mostly I wanted to go back into your womb before my life began, where I imagine it's warm and cozy and blissfully peaceful and far away from Dakota Duncan.

M, my locker was COVERED, and I mean COVERED!! with the pictures of me, pre-surgery.

Dakota must have used her phone to take pictures of my baby pictures (the sneaky snake!) and had them blown up to gargantuan sizes, and she pasted them all over my locker like some gross oversized jigsaw puzzle. And not only were they the pictures of me with my lip split from mouth to nose, but there were also pictures of other kids with serious clefts, and some were missing their noses! (Which has nothing to do with having a cleft lip or palate. Just so you know.)

Dakota had even scribbled in red lipstick, or maybe it was blood, "WILLA SHISBY, BOYFRIEND

STEALER" across the front of the biggest picture. (AS if!!!)

WILLA SHISBEY BOYFRIEND STEALER

I went catatonic after that, with all the kids making those horrible faces at me and pretending to gag. Seriously, at one point I couldn't even hear sounds. Instead, all I could hear was the sound of waves crashing around in my head or something, and even my sight got all foggy, like my glasses were covered in pizza grease or Vaseline or something.

Marley tried to get the pictures off my locker, jumping up and down so she could reach them, but she's so short that she could only get the lower ones. Luckily, Cody came by just then, and he was able to reach all of them. And he was spitting mad at Dakota!

Then the bell rang, and Marley practically had to CARRY me to her journalism class because my legs would no longer support my weight. I was too upset to go my first period class. And even though Marley is not a fan of "body art," she pulled up my sleeve and gave me a Spider-Girl semi-permanent picture on the inside of my wrist (It was a drawing of me as a superhero, complete with web and cape.), as a reminder that I can overcome any adversity that comes my way.

Her idea worked, too. Every time the memory of all of those kids making fun of me would surface throughout the day and made me want to cry again, I would just pull up the sleeve of my sweatshirt and look at the picture, and it would make me smile. (I'd also smile because Marley's a great artist, and I look WAY cuter in her drawing than I do in real life and with nicer hair.)

The only "draw" back (HA! Pun intended) about the picture is that I had to keep my sweatshirt on all day, even during gym class, because we're not allowed to draw on ourselves.

Although, it was Marley — not me — who did the drawing, and since Marley is student body president, that sort of makes her the boss of everything school-related, which means she can do whatever she wants. (Because, according to my dad, normal rules of conduct don't apply to presidents.)

At lunchtime, I was still mopey, and Marley suggested I go to The Friendship Bench because a new student had arrived today. Marley said he looked as though he could use a friend.

Boy, was Marley right because kids were avoiding the boy as if he had cooties or the plague or something, and all just because he was sitting in a wheelchair. From his body's position in the chair, I guessed (and correctly) that he had cerebral palsy. We had kids in the orphanage with "CP," (That's the shortened version.) and like me with my cleft, they considered the CP kids "hard to place." All of us "hard to placers" got pretty tight, so it doesn't freak me out to see a person with CP the same way it does for other people (i.e. Olivia and just about everyone else on the planet).

I'm sure you know this, M, but in case you don't, the word cerebral refers to the brain, and palsy is the weakness that affects the person's ability to control their muscles. Each person's situation is different, and not all kids with CP need wheelchairs. Some CP kids can seem "floppy." That's what the nurses used to say about Milly, that she had the floppy kind. At first I thought they were just being mean, saying Milly was floppy, but I looked it up online and floppy CP really is a thing. Little Joe (He was born weighing only two pounds!) had spastic CP, which meant his limbs were stiff and jerky. (FYI, I also thought the nurses were being mean when they said Little Joe was spastic, but apparently spastic is also "a thing" in the medical world.)

But here's a question for you, M. Why do you think it's acceptable to call an able-bodied person "floppy," but it's offensive to use the word "spastic?" (???? Must investigate further...)

Robbie has limited use of his hands and his legs, so he has a motorized wheelchair that he operates with a joy stick thingy using his right hand. He's also hard to understand, but luckily I developed a good ear for the CP dialect from my time with Milly and Little Joe. I've assigned myself his unofficial interpreter.

I'm not kidding, M, when I say that the guy has the best sense of humor! It takes a little while to get used to the way he talks because he can't enunciate very well, but the guy's mind is sharp as a whip!

And guess what else??!!

Cody Cassidy gave Robbie his hat. Yes! Really! The most popular boy in the entire school gave his hat to the new kid. It might have been because Cody felt bad that his ex-girlfriend totally annihilated me in front of the entire student body, but hey, if that's what it takes to help Robbie earn some street cred at Triton, then I'm happy to be the "fall guy." He even put the hat on Robbie's head for him, after asking permission, and then tugged it down over one eye, saying to Robbie, "To earn respect around this place, you gotta be a rebel." (There's now a chance Robbie will get detention for wearing the hat, but I have a feeling if anyone can get away with breaking the "no hats" rule, it'll be Robbie.)

That's all for now. I'm off to recount the erasers in my eraser collection (over 4,400, last count), which takes a while, as you can imagine.

One...two...three...four...

Willa

NOVEMBER 4, 4:15 P.M.

Dear M,

Have you ever had a really bad, awful, terrible, totally sucky day, only to find out that there are people in the world who have it WAY worse?

Today was one of those days.

It started when Oliva came to my room to tell me I got a letter in the mail. I'm sort of embarrassed to say, M, but every time I get an unexpected letter (Who am I kidding? ALL letters to me are unexpected! It's not like I have a million—or even ONE—person who writes to me.) But on the rare occasion something comes in the mail for me, I get excited thinking that maybe … just maybe … it might be a letter from you!

And I know that by admitting this, you'll think your daughter is not the brightest crayon in the box, but for a couple of years after I came to live with the Shisbeys, I stood at the mailbox day after day, waiting for the postman and hoping that I'd have a letter from you.

That all ended with the Chicago blizzard of 2010 when Olivia found me outside, frozen and shivering, telling me I'm a moron and you would never write. Then she added, "FYI, Willa, your nose has turned black from frostbite. Tonight when you're sleeping, all the skin and tissue will die, and your nose will fall off your face. Tomorrow you'll have nothing but a big gross hole underneath that unibrow of yours." Thankfully, my nose was still attached in the morning, and except for some redness, there didn't seem to be any lasting damage.

But with today's mail, I thought maybe today would be the day. Especially since the envelope seemed handwritten and not computer generated. Plus, my hopes were high because Olivia and Diane were both in my room, standing there, and sort of excited, as if they knew who the letter was from.

After the first few lines, it was obvious it wasn't from you. It was an "invitation" of sorts for me to tour a school for a "once in a lifetime educational opportunity" and attached to a colored brochure.

Turns out, it was an invitation to an open house for a LIVE-IN boarding school in Rhode Island! Yes. RHODE ISLAND! The smallest state in the entire U.S. of A.

small... small... small...

Rhode Island, a state that is so small that it's almost impossible to see on most maps with the naked eye. I'm not kidding. It's practically the size of an ant, it's so small. It's so small that map makers can't even print the name on top of the state because it would blot out the state entirely. That's why on most maps the name is floating on top of the North Atlantic with an arrow pointing at a teeny tiny dot to the left. And not to obsess or anything, but did you know Rhode Island's official state name is actually "The State of Rhode Island and Providence Plantations," which makes it win the award for the smallest state, but also the state with the longest name? (Not to mention the silliest — if you ask me — with that la-di-da "Plantations" reference and all.)

La-di-da

After handing me the envelope, Diane and Olivia continued to stare at me like hawks, so I had no choice but to give the "invitation" a once-over. Not that I'd ever agree to go to a boarding school, ESPECIALLY not one on the entire other side of the country! (Even though it looked Harry Potter and Hogwarts Castle-ishy with the gray stones and turrets and stuff.)

IMHO (That's short for "In My Humble Opinion" in textspeak abbreviations.) a boarding school is just an expensive orphanage where parents dump kids they don't want, but with better accommodations.

After I read the invitation part, I started to read the brochure because, as I said, Oliva and Diane were staring at me with some weird level of expectation, and I figured I needed to at least glance through it. But, M, the more I read, the harder it became to hold back the tears.

I'm a fast reader, and it only took me a minute to understand that "Highbridge Academy" isn't your normal everyday boarding school for normal everyday kids. According to the second page of the brochure, it's a school that specializes in students with "LEARNING DIFFERENCES" and promises that students will experience a

"TRANSFORMATIVE JOURNEY" during their time at Highbridge.

By then my eyes were teary and blurry, but I could still make out other words they used in connection to their students. The words, "IMPAIRED" and "HANDICAPPED," as well as DYSLEXTIC, ADD/ADHD, and SEVERE OCD. It was clear by then that the school promised to take less-than-perfect kids and try to "transform" them somehow into something better.

"Well, what do you think, Willa? We could fly out for the open house. Just the **four** of us," Diane said after I finished reading it, a fake smile plastered on her face and her voice unusually high. And I know it's not right to be a smart aleck to your adoptive mom, but, DUH, there are only four of us in our family of FOUR! So I couldn't help it when I responded, "Just the 'FOUR of us' in relationship to what? Inviting the neighborhood to join in?"

Right then, my dad came into my room (We didn't know he was home from work.), and he took the brochure out of my hand and read it lickety-split. And OH, BOY! Was he ever mad at Diane! His face turned super red, and he tore the brochure into a million pieces. He told Diane that although he appreciated the fact there are schools for kids with physical and emotional issues that I <u>WAS NOT</u> one of those kids. He told Diane my OCD was, in fact, MILD, and I'd probably grow out of it. He also said that having H-SAM (aka Hyperthymesia) is not a disease or a disorder but a condition that might lessen or even disappear someday, but that he hoped not because then I'd be as plain and boring as Diane and Olivia. (Who came in the room when she heard her name, huffing and puffing and saying in a whiney voice, "Who's plain? I'm not plain. I'm pretty. I'm not plain. Mom, am I plain? I'm not plain. Am I plain, Mom? Mom? MOM? MOM!!!)

Then my dad told Diane that he needed to speak with Diane, "in private," which means their bedroom, but the door has a hollow core. Anyone standing on the other side of it can hear.

Diane stood her ground. She said she had "my best interests at heart" and how being around other kids with "serious issues" would make me feel better about myself. "I almost hate to ask," my dad said, his voice sounded "tight," so I could tell he was still super mad, "but what kind of pretzel logic are you using to come up with that assessment?"

And, M, you're not gonna believe what Diane said! (And just so you understand the context, let me tell you that Diane weighs, like, a hundred and ten pounds.)

Diane said, "It's simple. It's all a matter of comparison, Ted. It's like how when I feel bad about myself because I've gained a few pounds I go to a Weight Watchers meeting. When I see those women tip the scales at two hundred pounds, I feel so much better! If Willa is around kids who are even more challenged than she is..."

That's all I clearly heard for the next five minutes because my dad turned on the radio REALLY HIGH while he gave Diane "a piece of his mind" before finishing with and at full Dad volume, "THERE IS NOTHING WRONG WITH WILLA. AND BESIDES, THAT SCHOOL COST SIXTY THOUSAND DOLLARS A YEAR, DIANE! SIXTY THOUSAND!!"

Let me state for the record that (A) I've never considered myself "challenged," at least not in the way that Diane meant, and (B) I seriously doubt that Diane's crazy comparison theory even works. Like, what, "I'll see your dyslexia and OCD, and I'll raise you Tourette's and mild autism." (Those are card-playing terms, FYI, when someone wants to raise the "stakes" of the game.)

Good grief! Does Diane seriously think anyone with a physical or emotional challenge feels better about themselves by hanging out with others who have even harder obstacles to overcome?

When it finally sunk in that Diane did not have "my best interest at heart" like she told my dad and instead was trying to get rid of me, the waterworks started. And it wasn't the quiet crying, but the noisy hiccupy kind where snot comes out of your nose. It got so bad, I had to cry in the bathroom and inside the shower with the water running so no one would hear me. (I still had my clothes on, which seemed to make perfect sense, but looking back on it was really dumb because I ruined my favorite black Converse shoes.)

I cried until I ran out of hot water, which is saying a lot, because our hot water tank is jumbo size. After I changed into some dry clothes, I noticed that I had about a million missed calls from Marley. With all the high drama, I totally forgot that I was supposed to go with Marley and her mom to the hospital. (Mrs. A is a pediatric oncologist, a doctor for kids with cancer.) Since I've been a little down lately, I think the hospital visit was an organized effort between Marley and her mom so I could put things "in perspective."

And let me say this: If you're ever the guest of honor at a rip-roaring pity party for one, just go to the pediatric oncology department with Marley and her mom, and you'll quickly discover that whatever drama is currently turning your world sunny side over. It's NOTHING compared to what those poor little kids go through while fighting CANCER!

Those kids are HEROS, if you ask me. Every single one of them.

Especially the little boy who, sadly, went to heaven while we were at the vending machine getting candy.

He's now a hero with wings.

Yours in grief,

Willa

NOVEMBER 9, 7:01 P.M.

Dear M,

I hate my feet. (I'm also not a big fan of my nose, my ears, my elbows, or my knees, but my feet are my biggest concern.)

I don't want to pin the blame or anything, M, but I had to inherit them from either you or my biological father. So, I need to ask — do you have cute feet or ugly feet? What about your parents? Or your grandparents?

Don't get me wrong. It's not as if I have some wooly gargantuan Hobbit feet or gross cow-hoof-looking toenails like those dog chew things they sell at the pet store, but my second toe is slightly longer than my big toe, and my pinkie toe is sort of squished behind my fourth toe. (Plus, there was this little tuft of hair growing at the base of my big toe, but I just used Olivia's razor to shave it off.)

OH! MY! GOSH! IS SHE KIDDING ME?

Olivia is now standing outside my bedroom door SCREAMING that her razor is COVERED in RAT hair.

What a drama queen!

I gotta go put out the fire...

W

NOVEMBER 17, 6:26 P.M.

Dear M,

Are you a dog person or a cat person?

OK. I just reread that sentence, and it looks weird. It makes it seem as if you're some sort centaur creature, only in reverse, with the front half of you an animal (specifically, a dog or a cat) and the back half, a human being — a "person."

So, what I meant to say is, do you prefer dogs or cats?

Personally, I prefer dogs. And here's why:

1. <u>Dogs don't need litter boxes.</u>

Litter boxes are gross, smelly, and disgusting.

Seriously, we flush that stuff down toilets if it comes out of our bodies. Why is it OK to have a cat poop oasis in a box in the living room? (Or kitchen or bedroom or any other ROOM INSIDE YOUR HOME!)

2. Dogs are fun to play with.

The important word in that sentence is "with." Unlike cats, who prefer SOLO activities, dogs can play catch (usually balls or Frisbees), and they can be trained to retrieve your shoes and the morning paper.

(Cats, on the other hand, seem to limit their fun to either string unravelling or laser chasing, if all of those YouTube videos are real.)

3. <u>Dogs love car rides.</u>

Put a dog in your car with the window down, and your dog will joyfully put his head out the window and let the wind ruffle his gums like a sail on a schooner.

Put your cat in the car with the window down with the wind gusting him with the force of a Nor'easter, and you'll need stitches and a new convertible top on your car.

4. <u>Dogs are adaptable to change.</u>

They're a "go with the flow" kind of animal.

Woof!

Cats are hypersensitive to their environment and dislike change. (And boy, will they let you know it. They're sort of like older sisters that way.)

5. <u>If you say "NO!" to a dog in a stern voice, he'll</u>

get his feelings hurt and try to win back your affection.

If you say "NO!" to a cat, he'll give you the stink eye and the cold shoulder and might even poop inside your favorite tennis shoes instead of using his indoor oasis. (In full disclosure, I have no evidence regarding this. It just seems like something a ticked-off cat would do.)

6. Dogs are easily trained.

In no time at all, a dog can learn to sit, stay, heel, lie down, roll over, extend their paw in salutation, and bark on command.

Conversely, it's a well-known fact that cats train humans better than humans train cats.

And just in case you need more evidence why I prefer dogs to cats...

When was the last time you heard of a cat leading the blind, sniffing out cancer, or alerting Jimmy's mom that Jimmy has fallen into the well and needs rescuing?

I rest my case.

Yours in dogdom,

Willa

P.S. And if I'm ever lucky enough to get a dog and experience dog ownership first hand, I'll let you know. So far the closest thing I've ever had to a pet was a fish, and it died.

NOVEMBER 19, 8:10 P.M.

Dear M,

Diane and my dad had another argument about me last night.

Sometimes, M, it's hard to be me...

And not just because of my H-SAM, which makes it impossible to forget the bad stuff, where it will continue to be fresh in my mind, a week, a month, a year, or even five years from now. Just as real, just as painful, as the day it happened. (Sort of like an old-fashioned vinyl record with the needle stuck in the groove, where the same lines play over and over and over.)

H-SAM aside, what makes things so hard is that I have to pretend that I don't hear my dad and Diane arguing about me. That I still have to be nice to Diane even though I know that she doesn't love me. Diane's not abusive or anything like that. She's never spanked me, and she doesn't yell at me. She'll nag that I left my backpack in the kitchen or that I forgot to take out the trash, but she's never been super angry with me. The same can't be said about Olivia, whom she's angry with daily. But the weird thing is that AFTER she's done being angry with Olivia, Diane gets all lovey dovey smoochie poo with her, and she's never acted that way to me, which is why you might appreciate that sometimes I wish Diane WOULD get angry with me because then she might want to hug or kiss me after.

But no. That doesn't happen, and instead, Diane treats me as if she's BABYSITTING me. (Where you can't be downright mean to the kid because then you might not get paid, but how you don't get all snuggly, touchy-feely with the kid either because then you might get arrested.)

I think if I had to sum it up, I'd say that Diane "tolerates" me, and that's about it. Not that it keeps my dad from trying to force-feed me to Diane as often as he can and with little success.

Goodnight,

Willa

NOVEMBER 21, 9:03 P.M.

Dear M,

I'M A GENIUS!!

Not officially or anything. And not in any way useful that might help me get into a good college someday. But let me say, I have come up with a BRILLIANT way to get my classmates to like Robbie, my new friend, the one with the cerebral palsy that I told you about.

Kids can be mean. And I watch the way they look at Robbie. Sometimes even scrambling to get out of the way when he passes by in his electric wheelchair, especially freaking out if he has a little drool coming out of his mouth, which sometimes he does. It's a common CP thing, and it has more to do with muscle coordination and sensory perception than excess saliva, which can affect even non-CP people, especially when they sleep.

Seriously, I'm a big slobbery mess when I wake up EVERY MORNING! Sometimes my pillow is SOAKED by how much I've slobbered in my sleep. (Come to think of it, it's a good thing I don't have sleepovers cuz that would be a definite turn-off in the friend department.)

Anyway, here's my plan. Are you familiar with the story of the "Emperor's New Clothes"? It's the fairy tale by Hans Christian Andersen about an emperor who pays some tailors to make him some magic clothes, seen only by the coolest kids at Triton Middle School. Just kidding! In the real story, only "wise" people can see the Emperor's magic clothes.

The thing is, the clothes do not really exist, but so many people get on the "band wagon" because he's the emperor and what he says goes.

The rest of the story doesn't quite apply to Robbie's situation because it says how the emperor continues to run around naked with everyone yapping about how cool his new clothes are until some smart little kid yells out, "But the emperor has no clothes!" (Kids say the darnedest things! Ha!) And then everyone in the crowd starts to say the same thing, that the emperor is naked until the emperor realizes that he's been swindled and he's been running around in his birthday suit the whole time.

The theme of the story is how pride and vanity can have embarrassing results and how honesty is a rare virtue. But I have a different take on it. I'm convinced that what the story is REALLY about is that there is POWER IN POPULARITY. And, if you can get one cool person to say that something is true, then others will start saying the same thing, and before you know it, a whole bunch of people will have changed their minds.

So here's my plan. I plan to harness the popularity of Cody Cassidy, THE MOST LIKED PERSON AT TRITON MIDDLE SCHOOL, to upgrade the "street cred" of Robbie Wise.

And believe it or not, Cody is 100% on board!!

100 Percent

Here's the deal: Cody has agreed to laugh really hard every time he hears Robbie tell one of his jokes. The way I see it, all the kids will notice Cody laughing and having a good time with Robbie, and they'll want in on the action, so to speak. Trust me, kids want to be ANYWHERE in the vicinity of where Cody's shadow falls— he's THAT popular.

At first, Cody was hesitant to go along with the plan, and I can't say that I blame him. Because it's super hard to understand what Robbie is saying, his punch lines get lost in translation.

Say what?

Cody said, "I just don't think it will work, Chicago." (Did I tell you that Cody calls me Chicago?) "If no one can understand the guy but you, it just won't work." Then Cody shook his head, and his perfect hair fell over his right eye, which is a great look for him.

When I saw Cody faltering, I had to do something that I hate, and that's BEG. I clenched my hands at my sides in frustration and nearly shouted, "But they WILL, Cody! That's part of my plan. The kids WILL understand him. Just wait. I'm working on something right now as we speak. Trust me. PLEASE!" And it came out all desperate-sounding, and I'm embarrassed to say there were tears in my eyes. Plus, I may or may not have tugged on the hem of his jacket like a sidewalk hobo begging for spare change.

It must have all worked, though, because Cody agreed to help. He even casually put his arm around my shoulder while saying, "All right, Chicago. I'll use this 'supposed' power of mine for good. Just let me know what you want me to do."

Now here's where the second part of my plan comes in. It's still a secret, so don't tell anyone, OK?

TOP SECRET

My plan is to sell my eraser collection so I can get the money to buy a voice synthesizer (aka communication device) for Robbie. Then everyone REALLY WILL understand him because, let's face it, there's a chance my whole, "Emperor's New Clothes" theory might be a total bust.

I came up with the idea of selling my eraser

collection the other day when I asked Robbie why he didn't have a voice synthesizer to help with his speech like Stephen Hawking had. I'm sure you know who Stephen Hawking was, right? He was that uber-famous theoretical physicist who they made that movie, "The Theory of Everything" about. (Funny story: My dad says they stole the movie title from him. He was going to suggest it as the title if they ever did a movie about MY LIFE. Because, according to my dad, WILLA HAS A THEORY ABOUT EVERYTHING!)

When I asked Robbie why he didn't have a speaking device, he told me, "Naoo ... mawn ... keey."

Usually I'm pretty quick to understand him, and I repeated, "No monkey?"

Robbie nodded his head, only I couldn't quite tell if he was nodding yes or no to mean my guess of "no monkey" was correct or not. Then he added, "Tooo ... spen ... siivve," which didn't help me a bit because I bet monkeys are super expensive and that's why only zoos can afford them. To help me understand him, Robbie pointed to his knee and said, "Naoo ... mawn nee." And then I finally got it.

"Money!" Duh.

Robbie's family needed the money to afford the synthesizer.

That's where I come in — assuming my eraser collection is worth enough. Fingers crossed!

I'll let you know how it works out!

Yours in optimism,

Willa

DECEMBER 1, 11:19 P.M.

Dear M,

I'm sorry about the teardrops on the page, but I can't seem to stop crying.

It's not about Marley or anything school-related. It's about how no matter how hard I try, I'll never be a real part of the Shisbey family.

The issue — this time — is the stupid family Christmas card that Diane wants to send.

Diane decided she wanted to send a photo Christmas card this year. You know the kind. It's not so much of a card as it is a picture with a decorative border, where everyone in the family dresses in ugly matching sweaters and those dumb Santa hats while standing in front of the Christmas tree.

Diane made the appointment with the photographer months ago, she said, and she ordered red and green plaid sweaters with bells and bows on them for everyone in the family so we could all be "matchy." Olivia pitched a fit about it and only agreed to wear the sweater if Diane gave her a hundred dollars to help "ease the humiliation of it," according to Olivia.

When the sweaters arrived, (my dad and Diane were at the store at the time) Olivia opened the package, and there were only three sweaters inside. We thought maybe one sweater was backordered or something, and that's why it wasn't inside with the others. But no, I looked at the packing slip, and Diane had only ordered and paid for three sweaters: two women's smalls and a large for my dad.

When my dad got home, he asked Diane, "Where is Willa's Christmas sweater?" Diane answered that she didn't order me one, and when my dad asked her WHY??, Diane got all nervous, and she sort of hemmed and hawed.

By then, everyone realized that Diane DID NOT want me in the Christmas card photo. I think even Olivia felt bad for me, which would have been a FIRST!! My dad told Diane that there would be no family photo without ALL THE FAMILY MEMBERS, and if Diane thought otherwise, "she had another thing coming."

My dad excused himself, and he took Diane firmly by the elbow and "escorted" her into their bedroom.

I heard some murmuring from my dad, and Diane replied, "Oh, for heaven's sake, Ted! I don't know what all the fuss is about. Willa can wear one of my old Christmas sweaters in the picture."

And that's why everybody on the Shisbey Christmas card list will receive a photo Christmas card with my dad, Diane, and Olivia, standing in front of a plastic Christmas tree wearing matching sweaters, and me, sitting on the floor in front of them in a ratty Grinch T-shirt, but covered by a mound of presents so high that you can't see my face — only a dark ponytail that seems to spring from the top of the highest box — and with the words on the card reading:

Merry Christmas!

From the Shisbeys,

Ted, Diane, Olivia, and **Wilma**

Yours in familial despair,

"Wilma"

JANUARY 7, 9:20 P.M.

Dear M,

Happy New Year!

The holidays (or as I like to call them, "The Hollow Days") are thankfully over. Maybe it's my H-SAM that makes them so hard to take because past holidays aren't just memories for me like they are for other people, but instead, the day stays just as fresh and vivid as if it happened this morning whether it happened one year ago or ten. For me, every crummy Christmas is captured in my full HD brain, every emotion and every action is crystal clear, every gift, or lack of them, recorded in my memory bank for all of my earthly existence.

I don't want to get all Harry-Potter-Living-Under-The-Stairs-At-The-Dursleys on you, but when it comes to Christmas gifts, I'm definitely the Harry to Olivia's Dudley.

Here's the breakdown of Olivia's Christmas gifts versus mine:

1. **Olivia**: Gucci Double G Canvas Wallet (Retail, $720)

   Me: Dora the Explorer miniature puzzle (Retail, 99¢)

2. **Olivia**: Neiman Marcus Cashmere Sweater (Retail, $235)

   Me: 1 skein (96 yds.) pink cotton yarn (Retail, 99¢) **FYI: I don't knit.**

3. **Olivia**: $100 Gift Certificate for mani-pedi at "Finger & Toes Nail Salon" (Retail, $120 — includes gratuity.)

Me: 1 bottle of Wet n Wild GREEN nail polish. (Retail, 99¢) **FYI: I don't wear nail polish.**

4. **Olivia:** Burberry Camel Check Scarf (Retail, $430)

   Me: 2-count pack polyester paisley bandanas — 1 red, 1 black (Retail, 99¢)

5. **Olivia:** Jimmy Choo Malene Lamb Suede Boots (Retail, $735)

   Me: Converse Chuck Taylor All Star tennis shoe (Retail, $49, and the best gift EVER!!) **FYI: My dad got them for me.**

6. **Olivia**: Blue Hooded Puffer Down Jacket (Retail, $129)

   Me: Blue plastic shower cap (Retail, 99¢)

7. **Olivia**: $100 Gift Card for Sephora (Retail, $100)

   Me: 1 Carmex lip balm .15-oz stick (Retail, 99¢)

8. **Olivia**: Lululemon City Adventure Backpack (Retail, $128)

   Me: Nylon mesh laundry bag with drawstring closure (Retail, 99¢)

9. **Olivia**: Annual pass for Disneyland (Retail, $399)

   Me: Mulan coloring and activity book (Retail, 99¢)

10. **Olivia:** iPhone XYZ To The Nth Degree With Hovercraft Option (Retail, $GNP of Most Third World Countries)

Me: Samsung pink glitter phone case (Retail $4.99) **FYI: It won't fit Olivia's ancient, first generation, horse and buggy, shattered glass front, iPhone that I use.**

There were a few other things, but nothing much worth mentioning unless you're really in to zit cream and mouthwash.

As you can see, except for the Dora puzzle, which has no relationship to a Gucci wallet as far as I can tell, Diane gave me a "same category" gift to the ones she gave Olivia. And to her credit, I opened the SAME NUMBER of wrapped items as Olivia, (although opening 3 individually wrapped #2 pencils is hardly a fair equivalent to Olivia's over-the-top and ridiculously expensive stuff.)

I could go on about the injustices in my life, but I don't want you to get the idea that I'm ungrateful for the things I have or the gifts I received when there are so many kids in the world who don't even have fresh water to drink or basic cable, for that matter.

In ending, I'll leave you with this New Year's quote. (I think it might be for the Chinese New Year, but it still applies.)

May the New Year bless you with goodness to abandon all vices and embrace all that are virtuous.

XOXOX,

Willa

FEBRUARY 10, 7:13 P.M.

Dear M,

HAPPY BIRTHDAY TO ME!

As of this moment, my "tween" days are over. I'm now thirteen, or as my dad says in a **totally** dorky way, I'm now the big "ONE-THREE" and a full-fledged TEENAGER!

thirteen candles

Did you remember that's it my birthday, M? I hope so. I know you have your reasons for giving me away the day after my first birthday (and someday I hope to meet you in person and find out why), but it would be nice to know that you still think about me after all of these years. That maybe when you look at the calendar and see the date coming up that you feel SOMETHING.

I don't mean that I want you to be sad or cry or anything, but it would be nice to know that at least you're thinking about the baby you had thirteen years, zero days, four hours, and six minutes ago.

Olivia tells me I'm delusional and wasting brain neurons if I obsess over why you gave me away because, according to Olivia, all I need to do is to look in the mirror and I'll have my answer.

Then Olivia notched up her meanness when she added, "And kudos to your mom for lasting an ENTIRE YEAR!" She calls our mother-daughter year together the "ONE AND DONE."

I have a strong feeling, M, (and not to brag or anything, but I'm right way more times than I'm wrong) that you DO remember you had a baby thirteen years ago. At least I hope it's true. I think that if I had a kid — even if I gave them up for adoption — that I'd remember their birthday. (And for clarification, I mean that if I was a NORMAL person with a normal brain, like most people, instead of being cursed with H-SAM.)

Like I said earlier, I'm not bringing any of this up to make you feel bad or anything. I was just wondering.

Olivia said I need to just "give it a rest," which is her way of saying I need to get over it. She also said life is NOT an AFTER SCHOOL SPECIAL and my birth mom isn't getting all sappy out there somewhere, lighting candles on a birthday cake for me and boo-hooing in her pillow at night, all pity kitty. Olivia said that, instead, she thinks my mom — YOU — are probably celebrating what a great choice you made and your loss is also Olivia's loss because I ruined Olivia's dream of being an only child, so now she has to share a bathroom.

But enough of that sad stuff. Now, let me tell you how I celebrated becoming a teen.

My dad asked me what I wanted for my birthday, and I told him I wanted a MILLION DOLLARS. Then he asked what I REALLY wanted, and I said, "TWO MILLION."

Dad said, "How about something within reason?" and I knew that asking to find you was in the same category as the two million bucks (as in, NEVER GONNA HAPPEN), so instead, I asked to go to Knott's Berry Farm, which is not nearly as lame as it sounds because it's NOT a berry farm at all. At least not anymore, although you can still get berry pies and jars of jam at their restaurant.

Knott's Berry Farm is now a SUPER FUN amusement park with tons of FAST rides. (Too fast, unfortunately, because they made my dad super queasy, and they messed Olivia's and Diane's hair, so we had to cut the trip short and leave after two hours.)

To make it up to me, my dad is taking me out to dinner — just the two of us — YAY! — to Nacho Mama's. Nacho Mama's is a great

Mexican restaurant nearby that Diane and Olivia refuse to eat at because they hate Guacamole. And I don't mean the avocado dip you eat with tortilla chips. I'm referring to Guacamole, the restaurant's pet parrot.

Guaca, as he prefers to be called, sits on a perch at the hostess stand and welcomes everyone who walks in the door by squawking, "NACHO MAMA! NACHO MAMA!" Personally, I think he's hilarious, but I can see why other people might find him offensive, especially with that thick accent of his.

Well, that's all for now,

Willa (aka the birthday girl)

APRIL 4, 6:19 P.M.

Dear M,

Today is cloudy with a chance of meatballs.

I'll fill you in later.

W

APRIL 8, 7:46 A.M.

Dear M,

If a lowly caterpillar can turn into a beautiful butterfly, why can't we do the same?

Sometimes I'd like to stop crawling on the ground, spread my wings, and fly away...

Willa

APRIL 10, 3:59 P.M.

Dear M,

d...

      o...

          w...

              n ...

                    D...

                        O...

                           W...

                              N...

d...

    o...

      w...

          n...

APRIL 20, 8:25 P.M.

Dear M,

I am NOT liking this "puberty thing" AT ALL!

Olivia says that's why I've been such "a downer" lately. She says it's hormonal, and I just need to "deal with it," and it's "the curse of Eve," whatever that means, but I believe it's a biblical reference. I think Olivia must have heard it said on TV because Olivia wouldn't know a Bible if it fell directly from Heaven and landed on her head. To think Olivia would read a book, ANY BOOK, thicker than a fashion magazine is a laugh. And even then, she doesn't "read," so much as just skims her eyes over the pictures and criticizes how the models are not as pretty as she is.

You know what, M?

I don't think I was sad because it was "my time of the month," like Olivia said. I'm sad because there's a school dance coming up, and there's a good chance I won't be going. It's a boy/girl dance, and it will have an "underwater" theme. Marley is the head of the dance committee, and it sounds as if it will be a lot of fun.

It's all everyone can talk about, 24/7. The girls are buying their dresses and making hair and nail appointments. Yesterday I overheard Dakota and Dallas saying how unfair it is that they didn't know about the dance two months in advance because "there's no possible way" they can find a decent dress in "just three weeks." THREE WEEKS?? Just how long does it take to find a dress? Aren't there, like, dozens of dresses in a shop? Don't you just try on one or two and choose which one you like better?

My question is not rhetorical. I mean, really, exactly how long does it take to find a cute dress? You may find this hard to believe, M, but I don't wear dresses.

AT ALL...

AS IN, ALMOST NEVER! In fact, the only dress hanging in my closet is the dress that I wore to the courthouse the day my adoption was final, and it's a girl's size 5. (And I don't mean a teen girl's size 5. I mean a toddler's.) I keep it for sentimental reasons.

Oh! Gotta go!

Diane is howling through the door that my backpack is on the kitchen counter.

Until next time,

Willa

MAY 2, 3:59 P.M.

Dear M,

OHMYGOSH! OHMYGOSH! OHMYGOSH!

I AM IN SERIOUS SHOCK RIGHT NOW.

I know you'll think I'm exaggerating, but I have all the clinical signs.

- ✓ Clammy skin (FYI: I've never seen the inside of a real clam, so I can't 100% confirm this. But my pits are sweaty, and I have a gross wet patch on my upper lip. So, I think it qualifies as "clammy.")

- ✓ Pale (In full disclosure, I'm always pale, so I don't know that I'm PALE-ER. Now I have a weird green tinge to my paleness that I didn't have before.)

- ✓ Rapid pulse (Not to worry you or anything, but technically I should be dead. Because, if I remember correctly, when you feel your pulse by placing two fingers between the bone and the tendon over your radial artery — located on the thumb side of your wrist, you're supposed to count the number of beats in 15 seconds and multiply this number by six to calculate your beats per minute... Ummm... On second thought, maybe it's multiply by FOUR, in which case, my pulse is still really fast, but there's probably no need to call the coroner.)

✓ <u>Rapid breathing</u> (I almost fainted from shortness of breath, but then, I'm noticeably out of shape. Maybe that had something to do with it. The brown bag I breathed into helped a bit.)

✓ <u>Nausea or vomiting</u> (I hurled. BIG TIME! And in front of "He Who Will Soon Be Named" to my morbid embarrassment!)

- ✓ <u>Enlarged pupils</u> (I look just like a wigged-out LORIS!)

- ✓ <u>Weakness</u> (A rag doll has better muscle control.)

- ✓ <u>Dizzy</u> (Definitely. Picture riding the Superman ride, Escape from Krypton, at Six Flags Magic Mountain, and multiply it a thousand times.)

- ✓ <u>Changes in mental status: anxious or agitated</u> (FOR S-U-R-E!! In fact, my mental state is PERMANENTLY altered FOR LIFE!) I know, I know... "Permanently" and "for life" are pretty much the same thing, but when you hear what happened, you'll understand the reason for my melodrama.

Here's what happened.

It was lunch break at school, and I was hanging out with Robbie. You know, shooting the breeze and stuff with him while waiting for Cody to show up so we could put "our plan" in action regarding Robbie and his jokes. The plan was that Cody would come over to Robbie and me when I gave the signal. Once Cody was close, I'd ask Robbie to tell me one of his jokes. I'd laugh because Robbie's joke would be hilarious, and Cody would join in. If the plan worked like I thought it would, the other kids would all laugh, too. For once, not laugh AT Robbie for being different, but laugh WITH him for being a cool kid with a great sense of humor.

When I saw Cody across the quad, I signaled to him. OK, so maybe it wasn't so much "a signal" as it was me jumping up and down while madly waving my arms and shouting, "YOO-HOO, CODY!" like a total goon.

When Cody saw me, he immediately started walking towards me. Dakota, who doesn't want Cody within spitting distance of me, saw where he was headed, and she tried to grab him by the shirt to stop him. But he broke free and was mad that she stretched out his shirt.

When Cody arrived, he said he "needed to talk to me," which any fool knows is NEVER a good thing and ranks up there with your doctor telling you, "Please sit down," followed by, "I'm sorry to have to tell you this ..." before giving you the news that your life is in eminent peril.

"Go ahead. No one's stopping you," I said to Cody, and my tone was snarky, now that I think about it. Then Cody told me that he couldn't tutor me this week because he had to GO SHOPPING with Dakota so he could see WHAT COLOR DRESS she was wearing to the dance so they wouldn't "CLASH"!! And I know, M, that you'll think it's stupid, but my eyes got teary and my stomach started to hurt because EVERYONE who is ANYONE is going to that dance. It made me sad.

I think I covered it up pretty well. No one noticed except maybe for Robbie, but I knew I could trust him not to say anything about it. I turned to him and said, "Let's hear what ya got today!" (I'll admit my enthusiasm seemed forced and over-the-top considering the circumstances.)

Robbie started to tell his joke, and by then, because Cody was in the vicinity, the MAGNETIC FLUX began. (Remember science and learning about magnets??) It wasn't long before Cody's north-seeking pole magnetism drew every south-seeker in the lunch area, which just about includes every student who has first lunch.

All the kids gathered around as Robbie began his joke, which sort of sounded like this: "Whaa ... shoood ... ahhh ... short ... syytid ... ghoosst ... aavve?" but what I knew was, "What should a shortsighted ghost have?" So, I repeated the line for the crowd, saying, "I don't know. What should a shortsighted ghost have?"

As bad luck would have it, Dakota had arrived, and she was as mad as a wet hen that Cody was with my group and not with her. She barked at me, "So WHAT, Willa?" with her nose up in the air and a disgusted look on her face. "You speak spaz? Is that how you know what Robbie is saying because you speak spaz?"

Everyone except Cody and Robbie started to laugh, and I realized that my plan to help Robbie — and maybe myself — get accepted by our classmates was nothing but a stupid dream. Dakota's words were a reality check. The cool and the uncool would never meet.

To prove her point, Dakota went for my jugular when she said, "What? You think Cody is your FRIEND? We all know your dad is PAYING him to go to your house. The only way you'll ever get a boy to go your house, Willa Shisbey, is for your dad to PAY HIM!"

Have you ever heard the term "SEE RED"? It's a state of heightened emotion when the blood rises and we become angry.

When Dakota said what she said, I LITERALLY SAW RED! It was like I was in a red mist that was swirling all around me, I was so angry. Angrier than I've ever been in my life as I stared back at Dakota with her makeup and her designer clothes, the rich parents, and a built-in best friend for life, a twin sister and mirror image, to remind her of how gorgeous she is every second of her privileged life.

What did Dakota know about hardship? Or exclusion? Or how it feels not to have friends— other kids to laugh and hang out with. Even in the womb, Dakota and Dallas had someone there for them. But not me. And not Robbie. Or any of the other kids who don't fit the mold of "normal."

Right then, I'd had enough of Dakota trying to ruin my life. I vowed to myself I'd never let her belittle or bully me again, and I yelled back at her, "You know what? Yeah, Dakota, I do speak spaz, if that's what you want to call it. I also speak blind, deaf, gay, black, and every other language of inclusion and compassion. You say I'm a dork? I'd rather be a dork and know that I stand for something than trapped inside a body poisoned by hate!"

By then, tears were streaming down my cheeks, and my shoulders heaved as I fought to catch my breath. Marley had arrived in time to see my meltdown, and she stood behind Robbie, holding on to the handles of his wheelchair, her eyes rounded with sympathy.

Dakota stepped over to Cody, and she took his hand possessively, her eyes locking with mine, a smug look on her face as if to say that she had won and that it was "them" against me.

Cody's fingers automatically interlocked with Dakota's, as if he somehow agreed with her, was more than I could stand, and I turned and ran, blinded by my tears, pushing kids out of my way without an apology.

"Chicago! Wait up!" I heard Cody yell as I ran. "Chicago, please stop!" he called out. But by then I'd crossed the quad and stumbled down the stairs, running past the math building and towards the girls' gym. Throwing open the door to the gym, I ran to the girls' locker room, collapsing against the metal lockers and holding on to my stomach with both hands while hot tears fell on my shirt.

OH, FOR PETE'S SAKE!!!!!!!!!!!!!

Olivia is at my door yelling that she plugged the toilet and I need to find her the plunger.

Ugh! The life of the lowly serf...

Stay tuned for the rest of the story because things are about to get CRAZY!!!

W.

MAY 2, 4:42 P.M.

Crisis averted.

But Olivia needs a lesson in "Toilet Paper Use 101." Seriously, just how much toilet paper does one need? She must have used half a roll. (Luckily, Olivia went NUMBER ONE. If it was NUMBER TWO, Olivia would have been on her own.)

Now, back to the story:

Anyway... the waterworks are majorly flowing as I'm leaning against the lockers, attempting to breathe, and feeling my heart break for Robbie, me, and every other "nerd" or "dweeb" or unpopular kid struggling with the horrors of middle school when I hear the door open and a familiar voice say, "So this is what the girls' locker room looks like!"

It was Cody!!

He followed me! INSIDE THE GIRLS' LOCKER ROOM!!!

(There weren't any girls in it except for me, but still.)

"You're not supposed to be in here," I told him, stating the obvious.

"I'll take my chances," Cody said, coming towards me. He stopped when he got to me, and he stood, face to face, as my heart walloped around inside my chest. He stood so close that I could smell the cinnamon scent of his gum.

"What do you want, Cody?" I said. "Why don't you go back to your girlfriend and just leave me alone?" My voice cracked at the end, and I suddenly felt soooo tired. And old. Like a 50-year-old lady or a grandma or something.

"Is that what you want, Chicago? For me to leave you alone?" Cody said. And I know that I originally thought the nickname Chicago was super cool, but in that moment I wanted Cody to see me as Me — Willa. A normal thirteen-year-old girl, just like any other. Not the freak with H-SAM or the nerd he had to tutor in math, but a regular girl who went to bed at night thinking of girl things.

I hollered at him, "My name is WILLA, Cody! Willa!" I said for a second time for emphasis.

"OK, Willa," Cody said, his voice soft, and when he said my name, my eyes refilled with tears. Why was Cody doing this to me? One minute on my side, but then not coming to my defense when his girlfriend tried to make fun of me in front of our classmates. Just whose side was he on? I thought he was my friend. But whatever game he was playing, I didn't understand the rules.

Frustrated and angry, I unloaded on Cody. Said things I'd never have the courage to say, not in a million years, but Robbie's welfare was at stake, and maybe mine. I'd made a promise to help Robbie, and I planned to keep that promise.

I told Cody he couldn't have it both ways. I couldn't be his friend if he was with Dakota. I told him he needed to pick a side. (And I prayed it would be mine.) Someone with popularity needed to take a stand for the kids on the outside of the circle. Someone with the power to make a difference. It wouldn't work if it was just me trying to help Robbie get accepted by our classmates. And if not Cody, then who?

Cody didn't immediately respond. He sat down on the bench beneath us, and he patted the space in front of him as an invitation for me to join him, which I did. His closeness was doing some funny things to my insides, making my stomach gurgle, and my mind was a jumble.

"You KNOW me, Willa," Cody told me. "You know which side I stand on." Cody's voice had gone soft, and he looked sad. He dropped his head and picked at a sliver of wood in the bench with his fingernail.

Then Cody asked if he could tell me a secret. And because it's not mine to tell, I promised I wouldn't tell anyone. I can't tell you exactly what Cody said, only that it was about Carter, his older brother, and also about something terrible that his dad did and how Cody was unable to stop it.

Cody said that he really admired me for standing up for the kids who couldn't stand up for themselves. That it was a "great" thing I'm doing, trying to help Robbie. He also shared he never really liked Dakota, at least not in "that way." He knew they weren't a "good fit." Not by a mile. But his parents and Dakota's are good friends, and they'd sort of grown up together. It just seemed expected of them to become "a couple" when they got older.

And it must be that the saying, "Confession is good for the soul" is true because the world suddenly got much smaller while Cody and I stood face to face and only inches apart in the girls' locker room while Cody shared secrets with me, his eyes locked with mine with a feeling of ... I don't know ... It didn't seem to be the regular friendship stuff, but it had a feeling of CLOSENESS, maybe. It's hard for me to describe it, but it seemed special. That's for sure.

My body flushed, and my stomach churned from Cody's nearness as he tipped his head down, his face almost touching mine. Believe it or not, M, I knew what Cody was about to do. I just didn't understand why he wanted to do it. My heart and soul screamed yes! But my queasy stomach said ... Maybe another time.

Then Cody dipped his head down a little more... He closed his eyes... AND HE KISSED ME!!

Say what?

Yes, Cody Cassidy kissed me!! Me! Willa!

And I know that cartoons show "fairy tale" first kisses with warbling birds circling the couple's head and fireworks exploding like the 4th of July, but do you want to know what REALLY happened when Cody kissed me?

In a million years, you won't guess. I'm probably the only girl ON EARTH with this story to tell when someone asks, "What was your first kiss like?"

Because... Here goes...

What did I do when Cody kissed me? Did I kiss him back? ... Did I faint? ... Did I laugh uncontrollably? ... Or start to cry?

NO!

Instead ...

Are you ready for it???

Here it comes...

I BARFED!!!!!!!!!!!!!

Or I hurled. Or I vomited. Or whatever you want to call it. That's what I did.

Not immediately when Cody's soft, Burt's Bees lip-balm-coated lips briefly touched mine. And thankfully not ON Cody or anything, but, like, seconds after, inside a trashcan. I think it was because I was so upset over the Dakota thing and so nervous being just inches apart from Cody. I could feel my stomach do that gross gurgle thing as he leaned in towards me, and then my throat constricted and I tasted bile, which meant only one thing ...

Pushing my hands against Cody's chest, I got up and ran towards the exit doors and over to the trashcan, forcefully vomiting inside the can. Twice.

And if it wasn't bad enough, Cody was there to witness my embarrassment and remarked, "Wow! Can't say I saw THAT ONE coming." Then the door to the locker room opened and in came Kirby, Lauren, Alexa, and the rest of Coach Patterson's gym class to witness my humiliation.

"MISTER Cassidy!" Coach said as Cody dashed out the door with a quick "Bye, Willa!" But Coach wasn't mad. Or if she was, she was over it quickly because Cody stopped running to bend down and tie his shoe, and when he stood, he pulled off his hat and used it to wave to Coach Patterson, who smiled and waved back.

I'd tell you I'll never wash my lips again, but since I barfed, that's not an option.

Yours in confusion,

Willa

P.S. What does a short-sighted ghost have?

Answer: "SPOOKtacles."

MAY 12, 6:06 P.M.

Dear M,

The school dance is just days away, and no one has asked me to go with them. Marley suggested I help with the sign-in table or the punch table if I wanted to technically "attend" the dance without "going" to the dance, if that makes sense.

I told her no because Marley had told me earlier that the sign-in table is manned by the 7th grade AP kids, and the punch table has a staff member guarding it to make sure there's no "funny business" with the punch. (Triton folklore has it that one year someone spiked the punch with goldfish — the swimming kind, not the yummy snack — and another year, what everyone thought was foam from the melting lemon sherbet, turned out to be a huge mound of spitballs!) Ewww!!

Then Marley suggested that I ask Robbie to the dance as my date. I know it's terrible to say, M, but it's a dance. The chances are high that Robbie doesn't dance. (Even though I have seen a kid in a wheelchair dance before. Not in real life, but by the character Artie in that TV show "Glee," where the kids never had to do anything in school but sing and dance as far as I can tell.)

And I know it's never gonna happen, not in a million years, not if I wish on every shooting star in the sky or I blow out a hundred birthday candles or throw a billion pennies in the fountain. A part of me wishes that Cody would have seen that despite the barf thing, I'm a decent girl and maybe ask ME to the dance instead of Dakota. Not as his girlfriend. But as his GIRL- friend, a friend who is a girl. (Or would the appropriate term be "female-friend"??)

Oh! Gotta go! I have something in the "works" that needs my attention.

Stay tuned for BIG NEWS! I'm on a mission to change the world!

XOXOXO

Willa

(OK, I just reread my last sentence, and I believe I've majorly overstated. It's not so much "change the world" as it's "change a single life" of someone living in it.)

MAY 15, 4:44 P.M.

Dear M,

Whoo hoo!!

Is it wrong to toot one's own horn? Because my plan worked!! It really worked! The kids can now totally understand Robbie with the help of the U-Talk voice synthesizer I purchased for him after selling my eraser collection. (Who would have thought tiny rubber pieces could be so valuable?)

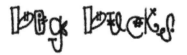

The synthesizer is super cool! It has different voice options, and it comes with a computer screen and a joystick that Robbie can use with just a couple of fingers. I gave Robbie the U-Talk during our lunch break at school, and Cody set it up for him in a jiffy. Robbie's parents were in on the surprise. My dad made sure that I got in contact with Mr. and Mrs. Wise to get their permission. They were SO THANKFUL that they invited me to a Shabbat dinner at their house. (I had to Google to see if Shabbat was, like, a special casserole or something. Come to find out it's not a "dish," but instead, a Jewish custom of celebrating the Sabbath. (Which is Friday in their religion, not Sunday, like it is for my non-practicing-except-for-Easter-and-Christmas-Christianish family.)

Cody suggested that Robbie use the British male voice option of the U-Talk so he could sound like James Bond, the spy in those movies, but Robbie said he wanted time to think about it. For now, Robbie's using the standard pre-programmed voice, which is sort of robot-sounding and with little personality, in my opinion.

And not only is Cody keeping up his end of the bargain by spending time with Robbie, he's even encouraged him to develop a "sit-down" comedic act versus a "stand-up," like the late-night comics on TV. Cody's even supplying Robbie with hats to wear at school so that Robbie can continue to be a "rebel" (Cody's word) like him.

It's so encouraging to see that with Cody's help (and mine, too, I guess) our classmates now see Robbie in a different light. Which just goes to show that if we take the time to see what's on the INSIDE of someone, then the outside doesn't matter as much.

Guess what else!

The "Armada" is giving Robbie his own joke column in the newspaper. Yay!! The name of the column is "Wise Cracks." (Get it? Robbie Wise... Wise Cracks.) I came up with the title, and I have to admit everyone thinks it's brilliant.

It was THE BEST feeling, acknowledged for doing something good with all the kids congratulating me. All except for Dakota, who, when she found out I sold my eraser collection, had to make a HUGE DEAL that as a thirteen-year-old, I HAD an eraser collection to sell. (Personally, I think she was jealous. Not about the money I got from the sale, because I doubt Dakota has money problems—other than how to spend all of her family's millions—but because of the attention I received and how nice everyone was to me and mad at her for not being happy for Robbie.)

In all the excitement of the day, I realized I never had the chance to thank Cody for all of his help, and even though the bell had already rung and I needed to get to my next class, I ran after Cody.

"I wanted to thank you, Cody," I told him when I caught up with him just outside the gym (and after I finished huffing and puffing and caught my breath). "Without you, I never could have done it. Without you and your power."

And you know what he said? Cody said, "It was you, Willa. All you." He told me that if it wasn't for me, he probably wouldn't have given Robbie a second thought. Not that he would have been mean or anything. But Cody said he would have seen Robbie sitting in his chair and felt sorry for him, thankful, that, unlike Robbie, Cody had full use of his "limbs," and could run and play ball and stuff. "Would I have stood up for him like you did? Sold my eraser collection to buy him a voice? No. I would have done nothing. Zip. Zero."

Then Cody walked away from me, and he was angry. Not at me, but at himself, I think.

"Cody, wait!" I yelled, and I ran to catch up to him. I wasn't finished. Besides wanting to thank him, I still needed to know why Cody kissed me.

"Why did you kiss me, Cody?" I asked, my voice squeaky-sounding and my body shaking from nervousness. Because as much as I'd replayed it over in my mind 132 times, I still had no idea why Cody kissed me.

Cody tipped his head, and his brown eyes held my gaze.

"I like you, Willa," he said. ... (**As a friend**, I'm sure he meant.)

"You're a good person," he told me. ... (You're ugly, I translated.)

"You're funny, and you're kind." ... (Which everyone knows means You're a total loser and not my type.)

But I didn't want to be those things: a good, funny, or kind person. I wanted to be cool and popular, and I told Cody that.

"REALLY, Willa?" Cody said, his eyebrows raised in surprise. "You honestly think being popular should be your highest ambition?" And when he said it, as if he was some all-knowing Zen Master guy and I was some shallow poseur, I felt my cheeks get red with embarrassment.

Cody explained popularity is nothing in the grand scheme of things. I'd been an example to others to do the right thing, not with an agenda in mind, but for no other reason than I saw someone in need and did something about it. Cody said that years from now when we go to our twenty-year high school reunion, people might say, there goes Dakota Duncan, the girl who USED to be pretty, but if I went to that same reunion, people would say "There's Wilhelmina Shisbey, that nice girl from Chicago who made a difference in someone's life."

And so maybe that's not what I ORIGINALLY wanted to hear from Cody (instead hoping that maybe he had at least a little crush on me, and the kiss wasn't just an "end of the race" congratulatory kiss for crossing the finish line), but his kind words filled me to the brim. I felt happier than I'd been in a long time.

Correction — I <u>FEEL</u> happier than I've been in a long time!

It will probably forever sting a little knowing that Diane doesn't want me on the family

Christmas card or that Olivia only *sees* me as her "sister" when it suits her, but I realize now I have plenty of things to be thankful for in my life.

I have a loving dad, who comes with a lifetime of free dental work, and I have plenty of food to eat. I have a nice house, and I live in a safe neighborhood that's just blocks from the beach. And the icing on my cake is that I now have THREE terrific friends — Marley, Cody, and Robbie — with hopefully more to come!

I now understand I don't need a bunch of kids to accept me into their group or their silly little cliques to feel that I matter. And I know that as much as I think Cody is terrific, I don't need him or any other boy to ask me to a school dance to feel better about myself. I'm just fine on my own. I also realize that what matters more than ANYTHING is the opinion of the person I see when I look in the mirror.

You might not recognize her if you saw her walking on the street, but you know her.

It's your daughter, "that nice girl from Chicago," according to a friend, the girl who made a difference in someone's life.

Yours in eternity,

Willa

Special thanks to the amazing folks at Kevin & Amanda Fonts for Peas for allowing the use of their amazing doodles. To download the FREE doodles used in this book, go to

https://www.kevinandamanda.com/fonts

The following fonts were used:

Pea Karen's Doodles

Pea Fruit Salad Doodles

Pea Bethany's Doodles

Pea Cookie's Doodles

Pea Deliah's Doodles

Pea Deva McQueen

Pea Family Joy Doodles

Pea Jiawei Doodles

Pea Jillybean's Doodles

Pea Lauren Doodles

Pea Panda's Doodles

Pea Kiki Doodles

Pea KT Doodles

Pea Stacy's Doodles

Pea Stacy's New Doodles

Pea Shelly Belley's Doodles

Pea Tisha's Doodles

Pea KT Puppy Love Doodles

SAMPLE CHAPTER:

Confessions of a Nerdy Girl:
NERDY GIRLS DON'T
A NERDY NOVEL: BOOK 2

CHAPTER 1

Here's a tip: If you ever decide to run away from home, you might want to actually *run*, and not stroll, in leisurely fashion, as if it were a lazy Sunday afternoon and you're out for your weekly walkabout.

"Get in the car, Willa," my dad demanded through the open window of the car. He reached across the seat of the Prius and pushed the door open, his black-framed glasses slipping down to the bridge of his nose.

"Sorry, Dad. No can do."

I continued down the sidewalk but quickened my pace, careful not to step on the cracks. Who needs more bad luck? I've had enough to last a lifetime.

Two lifetimes, if I'm being honest. Who else but a Bad Luck Betty has not one, but two moms bail on her in a span of twelve years? First my birth mom, one year and one day after I was born, and now my adoptive mom, Diane. I reached a fractured part of the sidewalk and had to jump to clear it. *Step on a crack and you break your mother's back …*

Dad drove the car slowly beside me keeping pace, the Prius nearly silent except for the sound of the tires crunching gravel. "It's not your fault, Willa," he called out. "Your mother's decision to leave has nothing to do with you."

I felt the first tear fall and brushed it aside with my hand. Darn it. My resolve to keep *calm and carry on*, the motto of the sign hanging above my bed, didn't seem to be working.

"Which one are you referring to, Dad? My real mom? Or Diane?" I hadn't realized I was yelling, but I must have been because Mrs. Webb's poodle ran out of her doggy door and started barking at me through the slats of the picket fence. "Charlotte, quit!" I hissed, thinking—and not for the first time—that Charlotte Webb is a lame name for a dog.

"Wilhelmina Eugenia Shisbey, get into this car, *now*!" Dad roared at me, and Charlotte looked up at me with a weird look in her poodley eyes that could only be translated as *Really? Your name is Wilhelmina Eugenia Shisbey, and you think* my *name sucks?*

My dad had never yelled at me before. Not ever. From the first time I met him at the orphanage when he came to clean our teeth as the visiting dentist, he's been nothing but even-tempered. He didn't even yell when his real daughter—I mean, *biological*—as Dad corrects me, saying I'm as real to him as Olivia, wrecked his car, or the time Diane spent five grand on that shopping channel for absolute junk.

Did he look pained when the insurance adjustor told him the car was totaled? Sure. Ticked-off when he found the Visa bill Diane had hid? Absolutely. But he never yelled. And *trust* me when I say I'd remember. Memory is sort of my thing.

"Willa," Dad roared, "don't make me get out of this car!"

I choked on a laugh. It was funny because not only does my dad resemble Henry Mitchell, the father from the old *Dennis the Menace* comic series, with his black hair parted on the side and those oversized prescription glasses identical to mine, now he was *acting* like Henry when he yells at Dennis. *"Don't make me get out of this car."* As if.

I took my dog-protection stick off my shoulder and walked toward the car. I tossed my stick through the open window before climbing inside.

"Care to explain, miss?" Dad stared straight ahead while he drove, and I watched the muscles in his jaw twitch.

I picked at the mangled cuticle on my thumb. "Do you want the big picture, or just the subplot?"

How do you explain to the person who jumped through marital hoops to adopt you that you wish you were never born? That sometimes the thought of getting through another day, even though you're just thirteen, seems like a monumental task and not worth the effort. That on most days the risks don't equal the reward.

Would he understand?

Or how to make my dad see the obvious—that the only way he may ever get his real family back is if I somehow disappear. That if there wasn't a Willa Shisbey there might still be a Mr. and Mrs. Theodore Shisbey, and their lone genetic offspring, the freakishly gorgeous and dumb-as-fungus, Olivia

Shisbey. Besides, it seems silly to point out Dad's royal mistake in adopting me this late in the game—eight years, eleven months, and two days after the fact.

"I'm serious, Willa. I want some answers."

I wanted some too. Like why women always have to open their mouths when applying mascara, or why an angry cat still purrs. But kidding aside, I know what my dad wanted. He wanted the sappy conversation where I tell him how I feel or what I'm thinking, and all that other emotional stuff that I don't do.

I cleared my throat and went for the gold. "Would you believe me if I said I was acting purely on instinct and too much refined sugar?"

Dad slapped the steering wheel with his palm in frustration. "This isn't funny, Willa. Were you really planning on running away from home? Away from me?"

In fairness to Dad, and now that my fight-or-flight reflex petered out and my sanity returned, running away was a rotten thing to do. Diane runs off and takes Olivia with her, and then I decide to hightail it out of town too. That's three women running out the door in one weekend. If I thought my abandonment issues were strong enough to warrant some serious future counseling, Dad's new wardrobe was going to include a snug white coat that ties in the back.

Dad turned at the corner and inched home, stalling for time. "Answer me, Willa. Why were you running away?"

"Come on, Dad. Did it *look* like I was running? Mr. Nabor lapped me around the block twice, and the man uses a walker. Running?" I repeated. "Ambling away is more like it."

"Waiting…" Dad said.

I put my feet up on the dash and just as quickly took them off when my dad gave me the stink eye.

"You're always saying I need to get my head out of my books and get outside for some exercise. Why couldn't I just be out for a morning stroll?"

"*Gee*, Willa," Dad said, the use of the slang sounding intentionally ridiculous. "I don't know … could it be I got the idea you were running away because of the pike and bundle you were carrying over your shoulder?" He jerked his head twice toward the backseat. "Very Tom Sawyer of you—if you're going for the whole 'runaway orphan thing.'" It was sarcasm at its finest, and I'm proud to say Dad learned it from me.

Pike and bundle?

Who knew that a salami sandwich and an apple wrapped in a red bandana and tied to a stick had a real name? And here I thought I was the nerd. Where does my dad come up with this stuff? I may be the weirdo freak as the thirteenth documented person in the entire world to be diagnosed with H-SAM (Highly Superior Autobiographical Memory), aka "hyperthymesia"—with the ability to retrieve all the stored information of my past with the accuracy of a computer—but even that doesn't beat the random stuff my dad comes up with.

"The *pike*," I said, using a British accent because the word seemed to call for it, "is pure practicality on my part, guv'nor." My dad struggled to keep from smiling. My British accent really floors him. I also do a decent Inuit, not that there's much call for Eskimo-accented English around these parts. I dropped the accent and continued. "The stick was to fight off Mr. Creely's pit bull, and the bandana has my lunch. I'd have brought my backpack, but it has a dirty-sock, baby-puke combo thing going on lately."

Whatever anger my dad felt evaporated, and he gave me a tired smile. "My Willa." He awkwardly patted my leg before maneuvering the car into our driveway. "Please don't ever scare me like that. Promise me, Willa, that you will never do that to me again."

I swallowed hard to keep from crying when I saw the tears shining in my dad's eyes. "Sorry, Dad. I just thought … I don't know. Maybe that you'd be better off without me. That maybe if I wasn't in the picture, Diane might want to come back home."

My dad pulled the keys out of the ignition. "What's happening between your mo— *Diane,*" he corrected when he saw my expression "and me has nothing to do with you, Willa. And I will never be better off without you. Never! Do you hear me?" He removed his glasses and wiped the corner of his eye. He put his glasses back on and leaned toward me, putting his hands on my shoulders. "Choosing you will always be one of the best decisions of my life."

"Scout's honor?" I asked.

Raising two fingers to his right eye in salute, Dad said, "Scout's honor."

I smiled back at my dad through stinging eyes. True or not, it was nice to hear.

BOOKS BY LINDA REY

TOP SECRET:
Diary #1 (Confessions of a Nerdy Girl)

UNLUCKY THIRTEEN:
Diary #2 (Confessions of a Nerdy Girl)

NERDY EVER AFTER:
A Nerdy Novel, Book 1
(Confessions of a Nerdy Girl)

NERDY GIRLS DON'T:
A Nerdy Novel, Book 2
(Confessions of a Nerdy Girl)

I Barfed on the Bus (Picture Book)

ABOUT THE AUTHOR

Linda Rey

Linda Rey was born with the voice of an angel and a brain so amazing she'll probably donate it to science. When she's not busy *fa la la-ing* from the hilltops or doing fantastical brain stuff in laboratories, Linda can be found at her computer creating lives far more interesting than her own.

To see all of Linda's titles for younger readers visit her website at <u>www.LindaReyBooks.com</u> and <u>www.NerdyGirlBooks.com</u> , or you can email her at linda@lindareybooks.com (And yes, that's her real email. Unless you don't have something nice to say, then no, it's not.)

Made in United States
Orlando, FL
24 January 2024